THE HOSTESS

A BWWM Interracial Romance

Jolie Damman

CONTENTS

Chapter 1

I was walking down a crowded, smelly street when I heard someone calling out to me. Turning my head to him, it turned out he was none other than a barker – a man responsible for picking out women in crowds like this one and inviting her to work for his hostess club.

I was walking with my head down, thinking about the future and what my life was going to be like if my university degree didn't help me with landing a job. Working for a hostess club wasn't my idea of making it in life, though I could see why so many girls like me ended up choosing that kind of lifestyle.

Lifestyle, huh? Not sure if I should be calling it that. The whole thing wasn't seen with good eyes by our society, and I didn't need something else to add to the stigma associated with the kind of person I was.

The guy stopped in front of me, panting. He needed to chill out. I could see why he was feeling a little desperate to make me work for him, though. In his line of business, he probably got paid by the number of women he convinced to work for the club.

The street was still really packed, and I could barely hear his words as he talked to me.

"Miss! I'm not sure if you've heard it, but our hostess club is inviting more girls to work for us. Payment is really good, and all the women that work for us are pretty happy with being here. I'm sure you'd feel the same way, if you give us a chance."

"I'm sorry, but I don't really need the money right now. Thanks for the offer, though."

Except that I did need the money. Power and water bills were beginning to pile up, and I didn't know if and when I would have the money needed to pay the next partition of my college loan. Still couldn't believe I had to take that loan. Everything would be so much better right now had I not requested it.

Dad and mom could not pay my college debts, and I'd found myself at an impasse. It had been either getting the loan or finding myself working in a club like that one, where women my age whored themselves for some money – and it wasn't enough to pay all their bills.

I supposed they didn't have a choice – like I hadn't had with the loan thing. That still pained my heart a little, making me wonder when I was going to be able to pay it.

And right now, I really needed to continue focusing on my academic career. That and achieving the promise of a good job in a good company. Gosh, why did working had to be so hard?

His hand grabbed my arm, stopping me. "Are you sure? Because this could be the opportunity of a lifetime for you, and I'm not going to be offering it to many other people."

"Yes, my mind is made up about it, and I know there ought to be many more people out there willing to work for you. But unfortunately, I'm not one of those."

His hand let go of my arm and I walked away from there with a smile on my face. I knew I was going to make everything right. I knew I was going to make my life better, the prospect of working in a nice office environment already making my heart beat a little faster.

If I could make it work – If things turned around in my life – I wouldn't even have to ever walk down this street again. It was just too crowded, and right now I really needed to stop letting that kind of thought ruin my mood.

I shouldn't let that sort of thing ever happen again.

But then I heard another pair of footsteps rushing to me again, stopping right behind me. I whirled around to meet them, finding the guy from before. He was panting as hard as he had been a couple of seconds ago, and I could tell that he wasn't about to give up easily. This guy was a little too persistent for my liking.

"Are you sure about that, miss? We could give you a test drive of sorts. You would work for us for a night, and if you like it, we could hire you. Of course, it's nothing guaranteed, and..."

"Yes, I'm pretty sure I don't need that right now. Now, if you will excuse me..."

I spun on my heels, but he spoke again.

"I can make the payment double of what it is. You would be making a lot of money working here."

I had no choice but to turn to him, finding his proposal a little out of the ordinary.

"Double the normal wage? For real? Or are you just talking out of your ass?"

He put both of his hands on his knees, bending a little as his eyes flashed. He might be thinking he really piqued my interest, but nothing changed for me. No way that I was ever going to work at his hostess club, with guys much older than me acting like they still had it. I wasn't going to let that happen.

I still had my self-respect.

"I can do that, and a lot more. You could become a queen in our club, and I'm sure a girl like you would appreciate that."

"Uhhhh, thanks, but no thanks. I really can't accept it. I already have a life, and I would rather keep it as it is."

"For real? Wow... I thought I had you, but I guess I was just getting hopeful over nothing." He took a deep breath and continued, "Have a good evening, miss. And if you change your mind, you know where you can find us."

I felt a little bad that I couldn't take up on his offer and work in his club, but it was either giving the possibility of having a normal life again another chance, or sucking up to men whose life I couldn't give a damn about.

And I couldn't do that last thing. I was a woman of self-respect, and I really needed to try everything before ever considering the choice of becoming a hostess. I knew it would leave a sour taste in my mouth – of the kind I would never be able to forget.

* * *

I opened the door and felt a cold, metallic, and somewhat round thing prodding the back of my neck. My heart rate sped up in a second, and I thought I was going to die. I whimpered when I felt the hand of a man taking me to the middle of the living room, his intention becoming clearer as the seconds ticked by.

"What do you want?" I asked, finding it unbelievable that I was getting robbed this evening, of all the times it could have happened.

I was so unlucky. Fate didn't look at me with kind eyes.

"Nothing more than what you are keeping here in your house, and I know it's a lot. I know you are rich as fuck and could be helping a less fortunate person like me."

His voice was deep and it sent shivers down my spine. I couldn't help but feel like screaming for help, but I didn't do it. Nothing good could have come out of that.

"Can't you just find someone else to rob?"

He guffawed.

"No can do, miss. This place reeks of richness."

I had no idea what he was talking about. My house was small and I still lived with my parents. Mom and dad were some of the people I most loved, and thinking about them now, I couldn't help but wonder where they were.

They had to be somewhere inside the house, right? But if this guy had managed to sneak in, did he do something to them?

The thought of that happening brought another wave of shivers down my spine, and I couldn't help but feel like kicking this guy in his balls.

I wasn't going to do that, though. I knew it would only bring me misfortune, this guy then probably squeezing the trigger of his gun and shooting me dead before I could even as much as get a chance to scream.

I breathed in and out slowly. "Alright, you can have it all - all the money, but please, just let me live."

A tear rolled down my cheek, and I couldn't believe how humiliating this whole thing was making me feel. It was one thing busting my ass off for a future that I could only dream of, and another to be witnessing it all getting destroyed right in front of my eyes.

The man prodded the back of my neck again, bringing me to my bedroom. I had a safe with some money in it. I had some money at the bank, but didn't trust them enough. I didn't feel safe keeping much of it there.

Call me old fashioned, but that was how I was like.

"Just need to turn the dial with the right combination," I explained, bending and reaching out with my hand to it.

"Don't take too long or I might change my mind about letting you live once this is over."

The guy was wearing a mask, so either way I knew I wasn't going to get a glimpse of his face. Just as fast as he showed up here, he was going to escape and leave me with nothing.

"Alright, alright. I'm doing it," I said while turning the dial to the left some ticks, and then to the right and to the left again.

There was a click and I pulled the door open. My money stacks once gave me hope that I could turn things around, but now they were all going to be wasted with whatever this guy was going to spend them on.

He was exhaling quite hard when I handed him the stacks full of dollar bills. His pistol was still pointed to the back of my neck, arms raised as he made it pretty clear that I couldn't even twitch. If I did, he would shoot me dead.

"You are not going to get away with this!" I heard a rather feeble, hoarse voice coming from the doorway. The masked man had left it open.

My eyes snapped to dad, who was dashing toward the robber with a large kitchen knife in his hand. Mom was right behind him, and her hand was covering her mouth.

"Father, no!" I yelled, but it was too late.

He was already sprinting to the guy with the gun, and the latter had no option but to pull the trigger then and there.

What happened a moment later was nothing but a blur to my mind, dad's body falling limp on the floor.

Blood gushed out of his mouth and mom had yelled something that at the time - and even now - I couldn't comprehend.

The guy with the black ski mask pulled the trigger three more times, and all the shots pierced her skull.

I screamed and went for the two of them. The guy in the black ski mask grabbed all the money stacks and hurried out of the room. All I heard then was the noise of the front door being closed.

I supposed I should find some solace in the fact that at least he didn't kill me, but I couldn't bring myself to think about the incident that way.

I cried and whimpered while pulling the dead bodies of my mom and dad to me. I sang to them a soothing, slow song while remembering all the good moments I shared with them.

My mind could not accept the fact that they were all gone now. I didn't want to blame my father, but it was all his fault. Had he not made the terrible mistake he did, he and his wife would still be alive.

And I wouldn't have to face a life without parents.

Chapter 2

"Miss, I hope you realize we don't usually do this. Giving another loan to someone who didn't manage to make the first payment yet is unheard of for us. I wish I could just give it to you, but I also don't want to give people here the wrong idea about us, if you catch my drift."

And I did. I really did, but now, more than ever before, I was desperate for money, and I had no idea for how much longer I was going to be able to continue living without more of it. I was poor before, and thanks to the jerk that robbed me, I was even more so now.

I had no idea how I was going to proceed from now on without more money. And I was thinking that I needed a lot of it – more so than I had back inside that safe where I'd kept those money stacks.

Not a lot of time passed since mom and dad were killed. I couldn't keep going on like this, scraping by every day and hoping that something favorable to me was going to happen out of the blue. Something worth calling this life good – worth living – but was that even something that might happen, or was I dreaming too high right now?

Some people could get the wrong idea, but this looked like a normal building from the outside. And from the inside too. I'd never thought that, one day, I would find myself here again – other than to pay him the amount I owed – I thought while shifting my weight. Just being here was making me feel so uncomfortable, and I was kind of thinking that this wasn't going to end well for me.

Another loan? From these guys? What was the worst that could happen?

"I know that you don't have any reason to lend me some more money right now, but I really need it. I think I might end up getting kicked out of my home if I can't finish paying my mortgage," I pleaded, my voice cracking.

I was on the verge of breaking down before him.

The man was sitting behind his desk, his hands folded on the surface of it. He was a businessman and he couldn't believe he was going to have to make this choice – either give me what I needed or condemn me to a life of misery and poorness.

I didn't know much about the guy, but I knew he'd been poor before, and that was one of the many things he wouldn't like seeing someone going through. I didn't want to get my hopes up right now, but maybe he was going to cut me some slack and give me the money I needed – under several conditions I didn't want to think about at the moment. I didn't need one more reason to feel miserable.

He sighed and stood up from his chair. His hand settled on my shoulder while he took me to the balcony of his room. There, he offered me a cigarette, but I was no smoker. I shook my head and he took the cue, putting the pack back inside the front pocket of his suit's coat.

He lit up his cigarette and blew some air through his nostrils, looking at the night sky and admiring the district that I'd been before – the one with all the nightclubs and hostesses clubs. It still didn't sit right with me that I might take this man on his offer, but at the same time, what choice did I have, now that it appeared that this loan shark was going to give me the thing that was like air for my lungs?

"Alright, I might just give you the loan, but you are going to have to promise me something – something I'm not sure you could do."

I examined his eyes and said, "I can do anything. Anything, really. You have no idea how much I need that money as soon as possible."

He blew another cloud of smoke through his nostrils.

"Guess I don't have much of a choice," he said, leaning on the short wall of the balcony and putting his arms on it. "You will have to pay me double of what I loan, and you will have to work in a nightclub I own. I'm not changing the offer. It's that, or nothing."

My heart skipped a beat. Of all the things he could have chosen for me as conditions so that I wouldn't just get his money and skip town, he picked those? I didn't know what was worse, if it was paying double the interest rate or working as a hostess in that district. I'd never thought it would happen one day. That barker was going to have a field day when he saw me again.

Fate didn't look at me with kind eyes, did it? It seemed it was intent on fucking me over and over again.

"Have you changed your mind already?" He asked, his fingers holding his cigarette in between two of them.

I smiled.

"No, I'm going to. Which club am I going to have to work at again?"

His eyes widened in surprise. He'd probably thought that I wasn't going to accept anything and that he would have had to find another woman – another idiot – that was more willing than me to do that sort of stupid thing.

Working in a hostess club... That was now how I thought my life was going to pan out once I was an adult. I just wished I had enough money not to subjugate myself to this kind of humiliation. He didn't see it that way, but it didn't change anything. It didn't matter to me how he looked at it.

It was either this or doing... I didn't know what I would be doing. To be fair, in terms of things that I could be doing right now, working as a hostess wasn't the worst option. I would just not be able to tell anyone what I would be doing, and I was going to have to double down on my academic studies so that I could have greater hope for a better future.

Anything to make it so working as a hostess didn't become a permanent thing.

* * *

I stopped in front of the building, unsure how I should be reacting. This was going to be my first day working here, and I could tell this wasn't the kind of place for me. People were walking here and there behind me, and I couldn't help but feel that someone would recognize me here and end all my chances of ever making it in life.

If my professors and colleagues found out about this, I was sure that I would get kicked out of college. Not in the literal sense, but people there would just stop talking to me – and that was the kind of thing I could not afford to let happen.

I needed as many people as I could have helping me – as many friends as possible, or else this whole thing was going to get out of control.

The barker from the other day stopped in front of me, his hand clapping like he couldn't believe I was here and that this whole thing wasn't some kind of trick his mind was playing on him.

"My goodness, miss. I didn't think you were going to change your mind so soon."

I sighed. "Me neither, but I didn't have a better choice. It was either working here or... I guess you don't need to learn about what is going on in my life right now."

"I wouldn't say it doesn't pique my interest, but you might be right about something else. What is happening in your life is your problem, and I'm nothing but a barker to you."

I smiled. He had a pretty soothing, calming voice, and his eyes were pretty expressive. He looked friendly enough, but I wasn't going to tell him any more than I already did about my life.

The fewer people here knew about it, the better. Though, now that I was thinking about it, maybe it wouldn't be too bad to make some friends here. Making friends meant some information about my past and present would have to be shared, but I was already getting used to the idea of letting that happen, for the greater good.

He offered his hand to me, but I didn't feel like taking it. Plus, it wasn't like the building was too complex to be walked around in or something like that. People were making a line in front of it, and the place felt crowded, but it was still nothing more than a small building located in the heart of this red-light district.

People of all ages and backgrounds filled this busy, smelly street, and I couldn't focus on anything. In contrast, when the barker took me inside the building, I couldn't help but focus on all the blinking lights, the people chatting, laughing, and then I thought that I didn't know if I was going to be able to work here for long.

"Follow me this way," the guy said, taking me to a smaller room inside the building and closing the door behind him.

There were some women inside it, and some of them looked at me with curious eyes. They were probably asking themselves what the hell I was doing here, and I wouldn't blame them for having that reaction. I didn't look the part, though I guessed the guy that took me here was going to see to that soon enough.

He was going to make me look like them, all makeup, and no substance. It wasn't all bad and at least one good thing was going to come out of it, though, I reprimanded myself. Few people would be able to recognize me here, once I was looking like a proper hostess. Either way, chances were my professors and fellow students didn't frequent this kind of establishment often, so chances of my life getting ruined for working here were slim to none.

Inside this smaller changing room, I could still hear some of the loud music coming from the main room – the one with all the couches, hostesses, and customers – but it sounded muffled. Knowing that here I could relax a little was comforting, and even though I was still going to have my first night out there in the main room, I was already kind of missing this much smaller space delimited by four walls and wondering what hour my break was going to be.

"Alright, Mrs. Malone. I think it's time to turn you into a different woman. A woman that any man in the world would fall for..."

I gave him an uncomfortable smile, which he ignored or didn't seem to have noticed. He went on.

"I know that working here can kind of be too much, but please don't worry about it," he insisted, dragging me to the other side of the room and opening one of the closets. It was big, housing many clothing pieces that I would love to try under better, different circumstances. I still hadn't finished swallowing the fact that I was going to be working here for the foreseeable future.

"I'm going to do my best," I told him, hoping that he was going to swallow that and stop bothering me about feeling bad regarding this kind of business line.

It took him no time at all to whip up something that looked nice on me. A beautiful, tantalizing purple dress that I was sure was going to grab the attention of many of the customers I was going to be serving. And an updo hair with a tiara that complemented it to perfection, too.

I then stood in front of the door that led to this changing room, my heart racing as if it was a speeding train.

The barker stood behind me, tapping my shoulder with his hand.

"You are going to be fine out there. I'm sure you are going to become our number one girl before long."

And given the amount of time that I was going to be here, working here, I was sure that he wasn't too far off on his prediction.

It just might become real.

Chapter 3

I sat down on the couch when a man, tall and imposing, requested me. Encouraging him to order many drinks and a lot of food from the establishment wasn't going to be too hard, though there was something about me I needed to control and keep in check.

My anxiety.

His eyes seemed to penetrate me like they were spears, seeking my soul. I had to admit I hadn't thought I was going to meet such a gorgeous guy during my first night working here.

I had no idea how a conversation with him was going to be like, and this being my first night here, I hadn't thought that it was going to be so different from what I'd thought it was going to be.

This guy looked at me with curious eyes, keeping his legs spread wide. And he was wearing an expensive-looking suit that highlighted his best features.

I had not thought that I was going to get a crush on my first customer. I was not doing this right, was I?

Here I was, sitting on the couch with him just hoping that he would tell me that he found me gorgeous or something like that, bringing his hand to mine and then-

Stop, Renae. You need to get your shit together and focus on your work. Or else your loan won't be paid and those guys will kill you. They are loan sharks. What do you think they do with customers that don't pay them?

I took in a deep breath and said, "So, wanna get something to eat? We have a variety of options and I'm sure at least some of them are to your liking."

His voice was deep and commanding when he spoke.

"Sure, why not? I kind of came here to see a gorgeous lady like you, but some food and a good drink would come a long way, too."

I shot my hand up, over my head, and waved it. One of the waiters noticed it and came to us.

"What would you like to get?"

I told him what we were going to have. A bottle of our strongest vodka and a platter of fruit. Nothing out of the ordinary, and I could already imagine what I was going to feel like once the conversation was flowing and he was telling me about his life. I wasn't his shrink, so of course he wouldn't tell me everything, but I still couldn't wait to find out about what his life was like.

His hair looked pretty sharp, cut shorter at the sides than at the top. His eyes, penetrating as always, seemed to hold me with a gaze that I'd never thought possible before.

My mind was vaguely aware of the other people sitting around us, the mood lights, the gloom, the smoke that hovered over the floor, the booming music, and everything else that didn't pertain to this incredible meeting I was sharing with him.

It didn't take too long for the waiter to come right back, his hand holding the bigger platter with the bottle of vodka and the fruit platter on it. He put it on top of the small coffee table that stood in front of us.

I opened the bottle and poured some of the liquid inside his glass until it was almost filled up. "Thanks," he said, grabbing the glass and making my heart flutter. Though I was supposed to be nothing more than his hostess for the night, his body, skin, and everything else about him was making me hope we could be more.

He sipped from his glass and put it back down on the table. His eyes studied me for a second before he grabbed his cigarette pack. Doing the following was one of the many things I'd been taught by the barker, so I grabbed my lighter and lit up his cigarette. Customers were allowed to smoke inside the establishment, so that wasn't odd.

He took a drag from his cigarette and then commented, "You are a nice girl. What are you doing working in a place like this one?"

There were two things from his affirmation I ended up taking notes of. First, it was the fact he'd called me 'girl.' I guessed that, from his point of view, it made sense for him to call me that, but I was still a little hopeful he wasn't thinking that way about me.

I mean, was the difference in age that noticeable? He looked a lot older than me, with a peachy skin that wasn't covered with wrinkles or any other defects, though he did have some of them. His eyes betrayed his age too, and overall I knew I was way below his league, but Jesus... I hadn't thought that was going to be one of the first things he would mention.

And the other thing I took note of was him saying I still didn't look the part – didn't look good enough to be working here, or just didn't look like a whore enough. I didn't know what to make of that last thing, so I didn't focus on it much.

I smiled and grabbed a piece of apple from the fruit platter, moving it to his mouth. I could feel the smell of his cologne wafting in the air and coming to my nostrils, making my heart melt for him even more. I was aware I was getting ahead of myself, having feelings for a guy that couldn't give two shits about me, but it was something I could not control.

He finished eating the piece that I gave to him, his stubble making me feel like reaching out and brushing my fingers against it. But I knew he wouldn't have found that okay, so I didn't do it.

I sighed and wondered where this whole thing was going to lead. It couldn't lead to anything out of what was ordinary in this kind of workplace, right? This guy wasn't going to begin thinking I was someone worth dating, and chances were he had a girlfriend that sucked up to him all the time. If I was thinking I had any chance this could pan out to something more – him and I becoming lovers – someone needed to whack me on the head and snap me back to the real world.

He finished smoking his cigarette and threw the butt on the tray, his action speaking a lot about him. This was a man that just oozed self-esteem, and that was one of the many things I valued in a guy.

Grabbing the glass of wine, he took another sip and put it down.

I needed to make some more conversation with him and continue to milk him, making him order more food and drinks. That was the only way to speed things up, to make it so I was going to have enough money to pay Oisin before it was too late. There was no way around it.

We talked some more, getting to know each other. The guy whose name was David seemed pretty interested in me, and time seemed to be flowing by. I couldn't believe how easy it was being for me to be making conversation with him. I'd thought it was going to be much harder.

Then, it seemed that our conversation was going to veer toward something else.

"You here by chance, choice, or because you are being forced?" He questioned.

Shock struck me, making me blink at him like a dumb fool. I hadn't thought he was going to make that question all of sudden. He looked worried about me.

I didn't think he cared about me that much. I thought I was nothing more than a random girl for him.

I felt a little intimidated by him now, my mouth opening and closing. I had no idea what to tell him. One of the reasons behind that was the fact I didn't deem it appropriate to tell him anything about my life right now.

Why the hell would he need to learn about that anyway?

I brushed a lock of my hair to the side, mumbling and making myself looking rather pathetic before him.

His hand looked for mine, setting on it. "It's okay if you don't feel like telling me anything right now. I was just making a question, and I know it sounded a bit stupid."

Once again, I mumbled. I'd made him order some more drinks and food. Overall, this was working for me, but I still couldn't shake the feeling that David was crossing a line that he shouldn't.

"I'm sorry once again, but you don't need to tell me anything if you don't feel like doing it. Just... forget that I said anything and let's continue that awesome conversation we were having."

He was actually enjoying it? I'd thought he was being generous and kind with me just because he was a gentleman and didn't want to make me feel like I was doing this all wrong. He was buying the drinks and the food from the menus, sure, but I didn't think he was doing those things because of me.

"It's... nothing that you need to worry about. My life is fine. I guess I'm just wondering about stuff that isn't there."

And maybe I was doing things that tipped him off somehow regarding my true feelings. Maybe I was looking a bit too nervous, and he was never going to invite me to see him next time he came by.

I took a deep breath and considered my options. I needed to do something about this uncomfortable situation I found myself in, or else this whole thing was going to derail.

David took another sip from his glass, in a moment putting it back down on the small coffee table. I then focused on the glass too long all of sudden, and I noticed I did that. Indeed, this whole time I'd been giving him signals that told him I was not quite here with him.

David was never going to request me again, was he?

The thought of that happening made my heart speed up like a galloping horse, and I quickly readjusted how I was sitting. I gave him a look I hoped was going to soothe his mind about me, and readied myself to make him a question that toyed with my heart.

He should stop worrying about me from now on and just focus on the fact that he was here to have a good time, and nothing more than that.

"So wanna another drink and some more food?"

His eyes widened for a fraction of a second before he exhaled. I guessed he was thinking there wasn't much he could do. If I didn't want to share anything of my life with him, then that's how it's going to be. David was a gentleman and he would never force anything on me.

"Alright, sure. No problem. Guess my throat is a little dry right now."

I breathed out in relief too. I didn't know what was going to happen from now on, but I sure as hell hoped that it was going to be something good.

Focus on the job at hand and on paying that loan shark once you have his money, girl, I told myself before pushing up the hem of my dress a little.

It was a skin-tight dress. I guessed that this was a common kind of dress here, looking at the women that also worked here and were serving their guests. Many of them wore similar dresses, though there were some that had put on somewhat peculiar models.

Some of their customers fumbled with their breasts, and I had to ask myself if that was allowed here or not.

The guards didn't seem to care, so I had to guess it was okay indeed.

The waiter came back with more food and another bottle of bourbon. It had been hours already since David stepped into the club, and he didn't seem at all ready to hit the road yet. I couldn't be sure of this at the moment, but I was thinking he was going to stay here for much longer.

Could it be he was thinking that maybe he needed to find out more about me?

I kind of hoped he was going to forget about what my life was like and act like the customer he was supposed to be – focusing on getting a good time here – but it seemed he wasn't going to do it.

I poured some more bourbon into his glass and brought it to his mouth. He drank it, his Adam's apple bobbing up and down. More than anything right now, I felt like kissing him and pushing him down against the couch, getting all cozy with him.

But as his hostess, I wasn't supposed to cross any line he would not. Without knowing what he liked and didn't, I wasn't going to risk anything. It wasn't worth it.

We chatted some more, and at some point he began to talk about his life.

He brushed his fingers through his hair and said, "I can't believe I'm going to have that meeting with that guy tonight."

Tonight? Then it wasn't going to take him much longer to leave Le Kissr. And I was kind of hoping he wouldn't. We were having such a great time together, now that he didn't appear to be worried about stuff from my life.

It took him no time at all to mention something else concerning his life, though.

"And I don't know how I'm going to approach the subject with him."

I had no idea what he was talking about, but I was still going to continue pretending otherwise. As a hostess, I was supposed to make him feel nice and comfortable here. I wished I could find all about him, what his life was like, and what he did for a living, though I guessed that last thing was going to come out sooner or later. It just seemed he had a lump in his throat he couldn't keep hidden from me for too long.

Chances were he was a billionaire, running a company that worked for him, that thought of him as his Master and treated him like a King. I wished I was his wife so that I could feel what it was like to have a husband with so much power.

Woah there, Renae. You are getting ahead of yourself again, and that is not a good thing.

My mind was right about that. I was thinking, dreaming about things that didn't pertain to my life, and that was not okay. It wasn't a good thing, and now, more than ever before, I needed to focus on giving this man a good time here at the club.

He looked a bit hesitant right now, his hand going for the glass of bourbon on the small coffee table, but not grabbing it. I wondered about what was getting him so worried. He told me a little about a certain meeting, but didn't detail it much. Now that I was thinking about it, I didn't know much about his life, and that was saying something. This was a job where I, as a hostess, was supposed to know what the customer was like. That was the only way to make him have a great time here.

Something troubled his mind, and even though I would love to find out what it was, that would mean he would have then all the right in the world to make me questions about my life. I couldn't afford to let that happen – at all.

"Sorry, this isn't working, but I'm kind of worried about your hesitation from before. I want to know why you didn't want to talk about it," he said all of sudden, making me cover my mouth so that I didn't end up gasping.

I hadn't thought he was going to bring that up again.

"I'm sorry. I don't think it's important at all," I said.

"You don't need to be shy, Renae. I know something's keeping you up at night, and I don't know how to put this... but I want to help you. I know you have no reason to be accepting anything from a stranger like me, but I promise you I'm not going to bite."

Did I just hear that right? He was telling me that there was something I was doing that was making him think he needed to do something – anything – to help me.

All of sudden, someone nudged him on his shoulder, making him turn his head to him.

"Boss, I think something is coming up and we are going to need your help with it."

The guy looked pretty serious, the one that was talking to him. His invasion of our solitary moment of privacy kind of made me feel a little envious, though.

I kept that thought in check, not allowing it to manifest itself. Most of all, I didn't want it worrying him. I didn't want David thinking all of sudden there was indeed something about me he needed to know.

Fuck. Why the hell was I getting bombarded by these thoughts and feelings while having nothing more than a somewhat long conversation with a paying customer?

"I'll be right there. Just give me a minute here," he said, the guy's eyes questioning if he should follow his order or insist some more.

But that was his boss. He wouldn't do anything he didn't approve of.

David turned to me and I knew he had one more thing to ask me. He wasn't going to get out of here without learning everything from me he could, and that was a kind of frightening realization.

The guy that was with him straightened up his back, turned, and left.

David said, "Again, I know I might be insisting too much on something you don't want to share with me, but I can see that your eyes are hurt. Your soul is hurt and I just can't see such a beautiful girl like you feeling that way and not do something about it."

"I-I-" I said, stammering. David shifted closer to me, making me feel even more uncomfortable while kind of hoping he would kiss me. My mind was such a mess of feelings and temptations.

None of the guards as much as flashed a glance at him. He could kill me now and they would not be able to do anything about it.

I was at his mercy, forced to do everything that he demanded of me.

Maybe it was knowing I stood no chance against his wishes that did it. I spilled the beans.

"I don't know how to tell you this," I said, taking a deep breath. "I borrowed a lot of money and am being forced to work here. I don't know what my life is going to be like from now on. I need to work here for God knows how long. That is the only way to finish paying all the money I borrowed. I suppose my only hope is becoming the best hostess here and making as much money from men like you as possible, but that is a thought that frightens me..."

His eyes softened up.

"Ahhh, I knew something was up. Who do you own money to again?"

From then on, we kept talking for a while. I ended up mentioning the horrible turn of events that culminated in my parents getting murdered, and remembering that made me feel like it was happening right in front of me again. A tear rolled down my cheek, even. He grabbed his handkerchief and wiped it off before one of the guards or waiters took notice of it. Had that happened, they would have fired me for sure.

I was so glad I was getting all of that out of my system, but I had no idea where all this was going to lead to. Was he going to help me with that?

It turned out he wasn't going to have a choice on the matter anyway. The guy from before came back and forced him to follow him. I took a look at the clock on my phone and let a smile creep up on my face. My shift had ended for the night, and now it was time to find out how well – or bad – I did.

Chapter 4

The barker from before stood in front of me, his hand holding a piece of paper. "Congratulations, you were one of our most successful hostesses tonight! You really managed to milk that guy, didn't you?"

I smiled, not knowing how to react to that news. I'd thought that this whole thing – working as a hostess – wasn't going to work out for me, but it seemed I'd been wrong about that.

The barker's smile was a radiant one, but the other girls seemed less impressed than him that things turned out the way they did for me. I grabbed the piece of paper and smiled. All I knew right now was that I was going to treasure it, and maybe even show it to Oisin to rub it in his face that I was going to make this whole thing work. I was going to get out of here with all the money he needed, and then I would owe nothing to him.

One of the girls mumbled. "Can't believe I lost to the new girl."

I could go right to her and tell right in her face that she should say that sort of thing to me – right in my face – but I didn't feel like antagonizing anyone here right now. That wouldn't have been a good thing.

I grabbed my raincoat and walked outside. The night was busy, with people perambulating on the street in front of Le Kissr. I took in a deep breath and remembered David. The man from before, the one that made it possible to walk out of that hostess club with a smile on my face.

The only thing I didn't like was him getting all worried about my life. Was that going to change how he felt about the establishment, maybe even make him feel ashamed of himself to the point of never coming back?

A woman trotted in front of me, complaining about something I couldn't care about. I didn't know what was going on in David's mind when he began to make me those questions, but I hoped they weren't going to deter him from coming back and requesting me again.

All I knew now was that I couldn't rely on him to show up again tomorrow night. To make more money – enough to make it so the barker would be astounded by my progress again – I couldn't rely on David requesting me often.

I slipped into my car and drove back home. For the time being, it was going to continue being my home, and I didn't have to worry about anyone taking it away from me. Still couldn't quite believe I was working in Le Kissr to make that happen, though.

* * *

My feet halted in front of Le Kissr, still unable to wrap my head around how much time it had passed since I first got here. Things were going well for me now, all things considered. I was on my way to making more than enough money to pay what I owed to Oisin. I just couldn't wait to be able to rub it in his face, that I was going to do good on my word and pay up everything.

The barker came running out of sudden, yelling, "Miss, there's something you need to see."

"Wait, what kind of thing?" I asked, but he didn't seem interested in answering me. He just grabbed my hand and bolted right back into the establishment, some people in the vicinity throwing looks of concern in my direction.

The barker rushed with me to the back of Le Kissr, and I couldn't help but wonder why he looked so desperate and fearful all of sudden. More often than not, he was a man that smiled and seemed to be having a good life. The way he was acting this instant was nothing short of puzzling.

I closed the door behind me, wondering what he was going to do now. If he'd taken me here, then it had to have been for a good reason. What that reason was, I was going to find out soon enough, I assumed when he stopped in front of a black van.

From behind said van rounded a short, skinny man with black hair. My hand covered my mouth before a gasp could escape through my lips. Of all the people I thought I would never see again in my life, he topped the list.

Those eyes... I never thought I would ever see them again.

And they were filled with hatred for me. Since we broke up, I'd thought that he'd forgotten about me, but it seemed I was wrong about that. He'd come here to meet me again and brush up on some old topics I'd presumed to have been long buried.

"Renae, it's so good to see you here," he sneered, approaching me and making me feel like running right out of here as fast as possible. But I wasn't going to do that. I was no coward and I could face someone like him head-on, no matter what happened.

"What do you want?"

He chuckled. "Nothing more than to see the new you. A little bird told me you are working here now, and I thought it would be a good thing to find out how you are doing. I might even request you, my dear hostess..."

The thought of him doing that frightened me. I hadn't thought he would ever have the guts to show up again in my life, much less to come here, of all places. And who told him about me working here anyway?

It had to have been someone from college. Maybe one of my fellow students who didn't like me much and ended up finding out about my former relationship with him. Whoever did it, though, just fucked up my life.

"I don't know what you are thinking you are doing here, but this is going nowhere, Troy," I said, spitting venom at him with each of my words.

"My little darling, but that's where you are wrong. I heard you are meeting someone new here, seeing a new man. How is he like?"

I took a step back. My eyes looked to the side, but I couldn't see the barker. I didn't know what got into him when he thought that forcing me to meet Troy was a good idea, but I wish he'd stayed so that he could see my reaction now. That would make him realize the weight of the mistake he'd made. Not that I would threaten him or anything like that. I was just... disappointed.

Shooting that thought away, I made a decision. I was going to have a long, profound conversation with him. No way I was going to let this slide. I liked him, but this was a mistake I could never forgive.

"I don't know what you are talking about," I said, taking more steps backward while hoping I was going to be able to get back inside and get one of the guards to save me. Troy was skinny and rather frail. He wouldn't be able to do anything against one of the hulking men that patrolled the inside of the building.

"But you do. You know damn well what I'm talking about, and you are fucking going to tell me all I need to know about the guy. His marital status, the number of his credit card, where he lives, what his job is – everything, and you are going to stop lying to me. If there's one thing I don't like, it's people lying."

I took a couple more steps backward. I was so close to getting back to the door that led out of the establishment. All I needed was to get to it, and then I'd be safe and sound from Troy. I'd be able to get back into the changing room, change into my hostess outfit, and then I'd have a normal night working here.

"I-I-I don't really know what you are talking about," I insisted, stammering but very much still keeping my composure. Troy was thinking that by making me afraid of him I was not going to fight back, but he couldn't be any wronger about it. I was going to fight back with all the strength I had, and then I was going to make him regret coming here.

I whirled around and bolted to the door, my eyes looking inside the establishment before I felt the touch of something hot curling around my right forearm. Troy, and he'd managed to grab me before I could get to safety.

My heart sped up, and I didn't know what to expect from this, and how to proceed from here on out. One false step and he could fuck me up here to the point of breaking my legs.

I needed to do something – anything that might distract him.

I considered screaming, and I did open my mouth, but then he covered it with his hand. "You are not going to do that," he growled, his nostrils flaring. I could feel his hot breath on my face, and it was one of the worst feelings possible.

Most of all, I couldn't believe he was making me do this. I'd thought that our life together had meant something to him. It seemed he couldn't even remember it anymore.

His head inched closer to mine. His lips were so near mine he could kiss me and I wouldn't be able to do anything about it.

"What do you say, my little princess? Are you going to do the thing I'm asking of you now – tell me everything you know about the guy – or are you going to continue pretending you can get out of this unscathed?"

The truth was, even if I knew a lot about David, I wouldn't tell him anything. Not only was David kind, he cared about my life. He'd been helping me so much, and I couldn't imagine what working here all this time would be like without his help and care.

Troy was an asshole, and he didn't deserve to know anything about David.

"Ahhh, so that's how it's going to be, is it? You are not going to tell me anything, thinking that you can get away from me," he said, breathing in hard. "Well, let me tell you something about myself I don't think you've noticed yet. I'm not someone that gives up easily."

His eyes seemed to smolder with a hatred I'd never thought possible someone could feel before. His grip on my neck tightened and I could feel as if he was going to suffocate me.

"Please..." I told him, hoping he still had some of the good I'd seen in his heart before, back when I still thought he was someone worth loving.

"Please what? You think that kind of talk is going to make me change my mind about this?"

I remembered I still had David's number right here with me. If worse came to worst, then I could just call him and get this all resolved.

While he was nothing more than my customer, he was still a good man and I knew he would care. Just like Troy once did, David would care and he would come to my rescue.

He shoved me down onto the pavement, and I stood right back up. I tried to slap him – to fight against him – as best as I could, but he just manhandled me like I was nothing.

He pushed me against the black van, grabbed a black blindfold, put it around my head, and then shoved me inside the vehicle.

I heard the door closing shut before realizing it was too late.

His hands grabbed a length of rope that he used to tie up my wrists and ankles. I couldn't move, but there was something in one of my pockets he didn't know about and couldn't suspect at all.

His hand slipped inside one of them all of a sudden, from which he grabbed my phone, killing some of my hope of getting out of this in one piece.

The phone wasn't that important, though. I knew I wasn't going to need it. I had an earpiece that was going to work wonders and allow me to get the rescue I needed.

"I'm going to get us somewhere private, where nobody can be a bother to us," Troy mumbled as he fired up the engine of the van, tires screeching while he drove to the nearest intersection. He took another road, and I had no idea where he was taking me.

With any luck, when he mentioned 'somewhere more private,' he meant that he was going to take me to his home.

While I could hope that was what was going to occur, I couldn't be sure. Having reached that conclusion, I remembered David's number and dialed it while mumbling it to the earpiece.

Thankfully, the sensitivity of the little machine was good and it picked up the numbers after some tries. I was then able to hear the sound of the call being made, but it kept going and going...

And it didn't seem that David was going to pick it up.

"Talking to yourself already, my little princess? Didn't think you were that fucked up in the head," Troy joked, making me hate him so much more, and wish I could snap his neck.

David wasn't going to pick up the call, which meant I needed to be a little more creative about this.

Some minutes later, the van went over a bump, and then another and another until they were constant. Troy was taking me to God-knows-where with the intent of torturing me until he got all the information he needed. The sooner I could reach David, the better my chances of escape were going to be.

Having thought that, I sent David a text message. The earpiece could read to me whatever message he would later send to me, so all I needed to do now was to wait until he found out about this.

I knew he was going to. I didn't need to worry. And all I was hoping, for now, was that he was going to come here before it was too late.

And that... might just happen.

* * *

The vehicle stopped not too far from where there were all those bumps on the dirt road. The smell of grass and wetness came through my nostrils. The noise of crickets told me that we weren't in the city anymore, but somewhere else.

I breathed in and out, trying to control myself. I was feeling as if I was going to have a heart attack or something like that.

Troy turned on his seat and said, "Wait right here, my little princess. I'll be right back."

He pushed the door of the van open and stepped out. The noise of his feet crunching the cobblestones informed me that we weren't too far into the countryside yet. That was good. It relieved me a little.

His feet distanced themselves from the van. I pushed against the door, but it was to no avail. There was no getting out of this, not without David helping me anyway.

He was the only one that could. I didn't trust any of the so-called 'college friends' to save me in my moment of need.

I was still all tied up, finding it impossible to loosen up the ropes. And without taking them off first, I couldn't do anything about the blindfold.

I supposed I could scream, but we appeared to be so far away from everything I didn't think that would have helped me much. I exhaled while hoping that someone – anyone – was going to come out of nowhere to get me out of this mess. But that was the thing. I didn't think or hoped that anyone other than David would come.

I could still hear the chirping of the crickets, telling me that I was pretty much in the middle of nowhere. I wished I could lift the blindfold a little to take a peek outside, but I couldn't move an inch of my arms.

I paused my breathing for some seconds, trying to listen to what was coming from outside the van. But there didn't appear to be anything coming from there. I thought I heard the distant sound of some rumbling. It could be that a storm was coming this way.

That would be just my luck, really. Heavy rain and thunders would be like the cherry on top of all this.

The sound of something rustling against some grass startled me, making me jump, but it turned out to be nothing. Chances were it had been nothing more than a rabbit or a squirrel running about, looking for food in the middle of the night.

I breathed in and out, trying to control my racing heart and thoughts. He was going to be here. I knew he was going to see the message, check it out, and then ask me for directions.

The earpiece buzzed all of sudden. I'd just gotten a new message, and for sure it had to have come from David. I didn't have many friends and none from my extended family cared about me. They didn't know what I did for a living, and didn't care enough to offer me some help with the things that were going on in my life.

I checked the message, my heart beating like a speeding train, but all that there was then was just disappointment.

It was a spam message. Fucking hell. Of course it had to be a spam message. Why did I think it was going to be anything different? I was so stupid. So fucking stupid.

I felt like punching the window of the van, breaking it into a million pieces using just my fist to do so, but I couldn't even move my arms. I didn't know what I hated more. If it was the ropes that kept me tied or the blindfold.

At least Troy didn't gag me, but that was like looking for a diamond in a pile of human feces.

I exhaled. This wasn't working well in my favor at all, and if I didn't do something about it – didn't find a better plan to be taken out of here – Troy was going to torture me and do God knows what else with me.

I threw myself against the door, but it didn't budge, again. Didn't think it was going to anyway.

All of sudden, the earpiece buzzed again. I didn't even bother checking it out this time. Chances were it was another spam message telling me to buy their cosmetic product or something like that. Should never have searched online for a new red lipstick. I knew the company behind the search engine was going to get that information and sell it to the highest bidder. The modern world was a box full of bad surprises, wasn't it?

Time passed and nothing happened. If it had been someone I knew – someone that cared about me – then there would have been another buzz. The person who'd sent the first message would have tried again, hopefully even attempting to call me.

Out of the blue, the earpiece began to buzz continuously. Buzz, buzz. *Someone was calling me!* And for sure it had to be David. He'd finally read the message and was now trying to do everything in his power to get me out of here.

I mumbled something to pick up the call and my heart fluttered when I heard his voice. David's voice.

"Renae, I just read your message. Are you okay? What is happening? Where are you right now?"

"Oh, David. I don't know where I am. I can't see anything!"

"Can't see anything? What, like you mean someone blindfolded you?"

"It's my ex, and he showed up all of sudden and put this blindfold over my eyes. He's keeping me inside a van and I think-"

Footsteps began to approach the van all of sudden. Maybe they'd been coming this way for a while now, but in my reverie, while talking to David, I hadn't been paying much attention to my surroundings. This whole thing was so fucked up.

"Renae? What is happening now?"

"Can't talk right now. Ex's coming."

"Renae-" he was saying, but I muted him. I doubted Troy would have been able to hear David through it, but I didn't want to risk it anyway. His hand reached for the handle of the door of the van, pulled it open and he plopped down on the seat in front of the steering wheel.

He exhaled, keeping the door open. His loud breathing told me he was probably covered in sweat. He'd been working on something that took a toll on him before coming back. I didn't know or had a clue about what he'd done outside, but it worried me nonetheless. I thought about asking him about it, but then decided to keep my lips sealed. No point in beginning a conversation with the man that kidnapped me.

He exhaled again more loudly than before and said. "Phew. I didn't think it was going to be that hard. But that motherfucker got what he deserved."

Got what he deserved? That was curious, but again, didn't think that probing into that subject would have been any beneficial to me. If anything, that would just make him paranoid and think I was on to him or something like that.

I was going to keep my mouth well-shut, for now.

"Hmmm? Not going to say anything right now, princess?"

"Is there anything that can be said?"

He turned on his seat, and I could feel that he was smiling. Chances were he was thinking he had me wrapped around his finger.

The van took off, going somewhere. I could feel the smell of grass and dirt getting replaced by that of pavement and buildings. We were going back to the city, and I didn't know why. Troy was almost making me feel like he didn't care much about what happened to me.

The sound of loud music alerted me to the fact that we were inside the city now, heading somewhere else. Somewhere where he would have all the privacy and time in the world to do whatever he wished with me...

He pulled up the van and said, "Gonna leave now, but don't worry. I'm gonna be back soon."

Shit. And here I was hoping I was going to have more time to talk to David and try to tell him where I was. He was still on the call, so unmuting and talking to him would be easy. The problem was going to be figuring out where I was.

The door closed and I heard Troy going somewhere else. People walked by the van, but none noticed that there was a woman tied-up inside it. I lunged against the door again, but this time, there was nobody nearby to hear the noise.

Troy must have taken me somewhere quiet in the city where not a lot of people lived or came to do whatever.

I unmuted the phone call I was having with David, my breathing returning to normal. I could do this. I could get out of here and then call the police on that bastard, finally ending this torment.

"David, I need your help."

"Wait, what happened? I couldn't hear you anymore and thought-"

"Look, it doesn't matter what you thought. My ex just kidnapped me and I need your help."

"Where are you?"

"Inside a van, and I don't know how much time I have. He wants to know about you."

"Huh? He wants to know about me? Who is he again?"

I breathed out loudly. "I don't know, but nothing of this smells good to me. I think he might be trying to kill you, or do something worse."

David exhaled. "I don't know what is happening, but I'm not going to leave you in peril. Where do you think you are? Are there any particular sounds you can hear?"

I pondered his question for a moment. I could hear the sound of funky music being played, and I could also feel the smell of pork in the air. It was quite strong, making my stomach churn.

I told him about those things. "Alright, Renae, I think I might know where he's taken you."

"Really? I thought I was going to die here."

"Don't worry. I wouldn't let something like that happen. I'm going to get you out of there soon enough."

"David... Thank you. Thank you for this."

"Don't thank me yet," he said before ending the call.

I'd never thought having this little earpiece would be useful one day for a situation of this kind. I did use it pretty much every day, though, to listen to music with and talk with people. I didn't talk with my friends and family often through it – who did that this day and age anyway, thanks to the advent of texting – but, indeed, I couldn't have asked for something more useful and suitable for getting me out of this hellhole.

Time passed and I feared that Troy would show up all of sudden, drive the van elsewhere and end my chances of leaving this situation before shit hit the fan. But for the time being, everything was silent and I couldn't even hear people walking on the nearby sidewalks.

There weren't even cars driving on the road, which was puzzling. Either we were on the border with the countryside, or Troy didn't take me too far from the original spot we were at – the one with all the grass and the smell of something wet in the air.

For the time being, all I could do was to relax some more and wait for him to show up. Easier said than done, of course, but I'd made a promise. I wasn't going to allow Troy to fuck my mind up again. He did that once, and it took me many therapies and shrinks before I was able to feel like a normal woman again.

I still didn't know why he wanted to find out all I knew about David. That was puzzling. David didn't seem to know the man at all.

* * *

I thought he wasn't going to come – it'd been too long already – but then, all of sudden, I felt someone knocking on the window of the van. I turned my head and felt his presence looming in front of me. The man I'd been waiting for this whole time...

Still didn't know him well, but the fact he was here was nothing short of heart-warming.

His blue, piercing eyes made me feel like jumping out of the van and kissing him as many times as possible. The only reason I didn't do that was because I was still tied up and blindfolded, for food measure.

I couldn't see him, but I knew his eyes were still looking at me with that same penetrating focus from before – the one I knew him well for. David was just that kind of man. He would never change.

"Don't worry, Renae, I'm going to get you out of there."

"Just be quick. I don't want to think about what would happen if Troy shows up now."

"Yeah, no problem. I'm going to do it before that comes to pass."

And I knew he was going to be able to do it. Knew that like the back of my hand.

He added, "I know a thing or two about lock picking. This shouldn't be too hard. Nothing more than a common van's door."

I was getting a little anxious, my breath quickening. He needed to do it fast before that son-of-a-bitch showed up. I knew I shouldn't be saying those things about his mom, but he was still a son-of-a-bitch. His mom had once been a whore, after all.

There was then the noise of something clicking. I thought that he was going to manage to do it now and then I'd be falling in his arms and he would be holding me and telling me that I was the most important person to him.

My heart was beating like a galloping horse.

But then, he stopped. He stopped and made me worry that something I should know about was going on. What that was, I was soon going to find out.

"David? Is something happening?"

"Uh-huh. I think there's a cop coming this way."

"A cop? For fuck's sake. How much worse can this get?"

"Don't say that or it might get really bad. I'm going to do something to lure him away."

"What are you going to do?" I asked, but he was already running away, leaving me with many tormenting thoughts.

My breathing was quickening and I felt as if there was a vine squeezing my heart. This was not good. Not good at all.

"Hey, get back here!" I heard the cop shouting, probably thinking his boring night had just become a little more interesting. He was most likely thinking he was going to have to arrest David. A man about his age with a black van here in this dump and trying to lockpick it? That was one of the things that would always raise a red flag in anyone's mind, after all.

I waited some seconds, hoping that he was going to show up and tell me that it was all going to be okay. But time passed and there was nothing.

My heart accelerated again. This could go so wrong and I was really hoping it wasn't going to come to that. All I needed now was some assurance that my king was going to be okay.

Footsteps approached the car all of a sudden. For a moment, I thought they were Troy's but then I heard the lock of the car being picked again.

David was panting when he spoke.

"Sorry that happened, but I'm here now and it's all going to be okay."

I sure as hell hoped it was going to be. Nothing would make me more afraid and madder than finding out that all this was for nothing.

Troy needed to be locked up, living the rest of his days behind bars. That's all he deserved.

There was a louder click and the door opened. I felt the cold air of the night kissing my skin. Then, his hands went for the ropes and he untied them. In a moment, he did the same to my blindfold, finally freeing me from this uncomfortable situation I found myself in. Or still found myself in, to be more precise.

He finished pulling me out of the van and I thought that this was it, that everything was going to be fine. But then I heard the noise of something coming fast to us. It had to be Troy! It had to be him. It couldn't be anyone else!

But then, my eyes landed on a small squirrel that cocked his head to me. It looked so innocent that I couldn't help but feel like grabbing it and bringing it home with me. Too bad that could never happen.

David's eyes landed on me, softening up. He was hugging me, keeping me close to him as if doing anything else would mean he would lose me.

"Hey there," he said.

"Hey..." I said, my voice nothing more than a whisper. His presence had an effect on me I'd never thought possible before, and I was probably making a fool of myself at this moment. David was most likely laughing on the inside, thinking that this woman that was me was dreaming too high if she was thinking she had any chance with him. I didn't, right?

I grunted and pulled myself away from him a little. No point pretending I'd be ever nothing more than a girl he met in a hostess club. He would never think of me that way, even if he didn't have a girlfriend or wife. For what reason would he ever come to the club if he had one of them? He was a gentleman. If he were taken, he would be spending time with them.

But knowing he was single still didn't change anything. David would never have eyes for a woman that worked in a hostess club.

Chapter 5

"I knew I was going to find you two here," a voice said all of sudden, coming not too far from where we were. We were still by the black van, and that voice... it was Troy's. No doubt about it. I knew he wasn't too far from us. And could it be he'd been using me this whole time to draw out David?

His nostrils were flaring, and he was looking at me like he couldn't believe this was happening. There was a mix of emotions going on in his mind at the moment that wasn't difficult to scrutinize. *She really dumped me for this guy? Really?*

If only he could know I had nothing to do with David – other than being the hostess he liked to spend time with – he would leave me alone. But that was without mentioning the fact that he'd been looking for David, too. Even if I were his girlfriend, this would be playing out the same way.

And now, David was with me and Troy had all the time and privacy he needed to do whatever he wanted with him. If the latter had a gun, he could use it now and there would be nothing about it we would be able to do.

My breathing was quickening, and I could feel as if the world was about to come crashing down on my head. Whatever had to happen here, it wasn't going to be good.

Troy kept his distance for now, though. What was he planning on doing? Kill both of us? That would be too simple, and I was suspecting that his plans for me were a bit more involved than that.

But his hand didn't go for the waist of his pants. It could be he hadn't brought any gun with him, which would be nice. That would mean David could wipe the floor with him, making him think twice before ever showing up his face again.

My hand looked for David's confident, muscle-bound arm. Perhaps I was crossing a line here, but I couldn't imagine myself doing anything different at the moment. He didn't turn his head down and look at me, though. He kept his eyes trained ahead. If Troy tried anything funny, I was sure this hulk of a man wouldn't allow him to finish it.

David was worried about me, more so than he probably should, I thought when quirking up a corner of my lips.

"My little princess is thinking she's someone else, just because she's dating a white rich boy now!"

"That has nothing to do with anything, and I'm not dating him!"

"Ha! You are not going to tell me his name at least?"

"Why do you want to know his name?" I asked.

Troy opened his mouth, but it was David who spoke.

"Why are you chasing after me?"

"Hmmmm, I don't think I should answer that."

"Are you working for someone?"

Troy opened a smirk. "I don't think I can answer that."

Gosh. How could I have ever thought Troy was a good man. He was being such an asshole now it was unbelievable that once I'd dated him. I felt like skinning myself so that I didn't have to remember the fact he'd once touched it many times with his greasy, gross hands.

"You are wasting your time here, Troy. I'm going to leave with Renae, and there's nothing about that you can do."

"Hmmmm, but again, I don't think I need to do anything. I'm here to give you a good beating – something that you are going to remember me by, and then I'm going to get all the information out of you I need. Spoiler alert, though: I can't kill you."

So that's why he didn't bring a gun with him. Troy was here to kidnap David, and he was working under the orders of someone that hid behind the shadows. Who that could be, I didn't know. If there was a person that could know that, it was David. Problem was, I didn't think he was feeling like telling me about it right now.

He was going to keep his lips shut. It wasn't that I thought I needed to know about it or something like that. I was just worried about his well-being at the moment. Nothing more than that.

Troy said, "You might be thinking that because I'm skinny and you are all muscles, that beating me is going to be easy. But I can assure you that is not going to be the case. I'm going to beat the shit out of you, and once I'm done here, I'll be bringing you straight to my boss."

His boss. I couldn't believe he was being someone's bitch for the sole purpose of doing this – kidnapping the woman he said he once loved with the intent of luring out the man he suspected I was dating.

He couldn't be any more mistaken about the latter...

I stepped forward and stood in front of David. "You are not going to do anything. If you are thinking you are going to harm him, then let me tell you this – David is just my customer and I'd never let anyone kidnap him like you did to me."

"Ahhh, so there it is. The love, the care. You really care about him, don't you? You'd do things for him you never did for me. Should never have thought you were anything more than a whore..."

David then pushed me to the side, his eyes meeting mine. "I'm the one he's looking for, and I'm going to be the one dealing with this."

"Wait, you don't–"

But his hand sealed my mouth shut all of sudden, covering it. "I don't know the full details of what is happening here, but I know this guy is willing to harm you to get to me. I'm going to deal with him, and then I'm going to make him regret ever even approaching you again."

Those words, the way he said them... There was denying David cared about me. I just wished I could step in and be the one wiping the floor with Troy. The asshole's mocking smile was still making me hate the fact we had sex.

Had I been a more attentive woman back then, that would never have happened.

I'd have stopped him – realized that he was nothing more than a devil hiding under the guise of a sheep.

Troy lunged, shouting, "I'm going to end all this shit right now, and I'm going to make Renae realize just how important for her I am."

"You are not touching her ever again!" David shouted, lunging ahead as well.

There was a clash of fists, each man trying to push the other, hugging each other and grunting. Sweat broke out on their foreheads, and I gasped when Troy managed to land a solid blow on the only man I cared about in my life at the moment.

David struggled to get back on his feet. Troy tried to kick him, but the first managed to dodge his foot. He swept his legs, the connection making Troy fall flat on his ass. He grunted and pushed himself back on his feet in a heartbeat. This wasn't going to be a fight easy for the both of them.

And I needed to interfere, do something that would tip the scales in David's favor. There had to be something that I could do. Anything to give him the edge he was looking for here. David was rather stubborn and wasn't thinking about it, but he did need my help – more so than ever before.

Fist met bone, blood gushed out in the air, and looking to the side and the other, I couldn't see anyone coming this way. Either there was nobody here right now, living here, or people thought that it wouldn't be worth getting involved in a fight they didn't have anything to do with.

David seemed to be getting the upper hand, though, landing more solid punches that made me feel like cheering. But I didn't do that because it wouldn't have been appropriate, and I didn't want to run the risk of stealing his attention from the fight he was having.

Troy, out of the blue, swept his right leg and made David fall flat on his ass. His foot moved in a flash, pinning the first down hard on the floor. A gasp escaped my lips. If there was a moment David needed my help, then it was now.

I didn't know what I was going to do, but I wasn't going to allow that bastard to get away with it. I was going to save David before something bad and regrettable happened. Before he got kidnapped too.

I bolted to the both of them. "What the-" Troy muttered, snapping his head to me. He raised his fist, but it was too late for him. I threw myself against him then, bringing us both down on the hard ground.

David stood back up in a flash, pulling me from Troy. His eyes met mine and I saw a mixture of thankfulness and worry in them. He'd worried that I was about to do something stupid. And he was right about that. What I did was stupid, but still very much worth it.

"Fucking piece of shit. Should have known this bitch was going to do that," Troy grumbled as he attempted to stand up.

But David wasn't going to allow him to do that. He lifted his foot and pressed it against his chest, pinning him hard on the floor. A gasp escaped his lips, his eyes shooting wide in an instant.

David then pushed me to the side a little and said, "Let me handle the rest of this."

And he did. I didn't know what the move was called, but he immobilized Troy as if he was nothing. It had to be something he learned from judo or something of the sort.

Troy grunted, struggling to break free. But there was no getting away from this, and if he were a smart man, he'd stop doing that before David killed him.

Before he died...

I didn't know why, but the thought of that happening made me scream then and there. I knew I was in the wrong, but I didn't want David getting his hands dirty with Troy's blood. That wouldn't have been a good thing, and I was sure he would later regret it a lot.

His eyes found mine. They were filled with hatred. I knew he cared about me, but not to the point of killing someone else. David was no normal man, and I'd do well to keep that in mind.

"Don't worry. I'm going to finish this now, and it's going to be as if nothing happened."

And he did, tightening his hug on Troy all of sudden, the strength he employed intense enough to make the latter's bones make a crushing noise. His eyes lost all the light they had, but his chest was still heaving. Still alive. Now, we were going to have to do something about him.

Call the police. They'd put him behind bars and he'd never be a bother to my life ever again. That's what we needed to do here.

I gripped David's arm again, bringing myself closer to him. He looped an arm around me, and that was when I knew I was with a man that would do everything and anything to keep me safe.

His hands, his cologne, and the warmth of his body made me feel safe like nothing before ever did. Not even Troy, who I'd once loved managed to make me feel like this. I was with him now, and nothing and no one could ever make me feel afraid.

"I think we need to call the police. Not sure if they would arrest him, though," he said.

"Why... not?"

"Not enough evidence. My word against his, I think they would still keep him behind bars for some time, though – but that is a shot in the dark. And next time-screw that. There isn't going to be a next time. No matter what happens from now on, I'm going to keep you safe."

* * *

We called the police on him and they did arrest him, though there were a lot of things we ended up having to explain regarding our presence. We told them everything they needed to know, including the fact Troy was my ex and that he wanted to find out all he could about David. The latter was nothing more than a businessman, though. He ran a company called LifeSolutions, selling all kinds of medicines to the market.

With Troy behind bars, I could live a normal life – for the time being. I didn't know when he would be taken out, though. If he didn't lie when he said someone had hired him to do what he did, then that person was going to pull some strings. He was going to do everything in his power to get him out of jail.

I was in my bedroom, thinking about David. He still came to the club almost every night, but sharing those moments with him wasn't enough. I needed more. I needed to feel his arms, his hands pulling me to him, his hot kiss on my neck. I'd do pretty much anything and everything to make that happen.

I just... didn't have the courage to do that. Didn't know what he would think of me. David cared about me, but still... it was better not to force anything on him, or make him think that, indeed, I was a slut.

I had my phone in my hands. Pressing some buttons, it didn't take me long to find his profile on Instagram. And my goodness, did he look like a man ready to take on the whole world and win!

He had a couple of photos of himself, but no woman. Not even a single one. The thought of what that could mean made my heart beat a little faster. But in a moment I put it back into its place. No point thinking he would ever think of me as anything more than the cute, smarty hostess that always made him have a good time.

I killed the screen of the phone and put it away. No point wasting time with things I had no control over, even if the thought of finding the right path to his heart was a little too tempting for me right now.

I imagined that happening one day, his lips then telling me I was the most beautiful woman ever in the world for him, his hands cupping my cheeks before he delivered a powerful kiss that would make my heart melt.

I sighed. No point in thinking that sort of thing had any chance of happening. There just wasn't, and I'd do well to keep that in mind.

I closed my eyes and thought that for sure I was going to sleep, but it appeared to me this was going to be another insomnia-driven night. *Damn it!* I thought while hoping a scientist somewhere would, one day, find something that would make it impossible for me to think much. The heart of my sleepless night problems was the fact I thought too much sometimes.

It wouldn't be much longer now until I made enough money in Le Kissr to pay off Oisin. I couldn't wait for the day that would happen, and it would all be thanks to the only man in this world that cared for me.

He stood up for me and stopped that son of a bitch that was my ex from doing something terrible – something that would make me think that life wasn't worth the hassle after all, that it wasn't worth living.

I sighed and grabbed the phone once more. I was making a big mistake doing this, but the fact was that I just couldn't stop thinking about that man, and there were still many photos on his online account I hadn't checked yet.

And my mind kept mulling that thought over and over. What if he had something that could tell me something else about him that would change forever how I looked at him? The thought of that happening was rather tempting.

Having thought that, I went to his profile again and thumbed the screen until I reached the very first photo he posted. It was first uploaded years ago, back when he appeared to be someone else. There was no denying the man I now knew was there, in the making, but he still looked so different then.

So much younger, but not as experienced as the hulking man that stole my thoughts and kept them to himself.

I felt a tingle of excitement running through my pussy. I know I didn't have any chance, but what if we began to date? Maybe he could take me out some time for dinner, do something together with me...

The thought was so tempting I couldn't control my impulse. I knew I might be doing the wrong thing here and-

Wait a damn minute. What the fuck was this new notification at the top of my screen? My heartbeat rate sped up for a moment, but then it calmed down. It was probably nothing more than a college friend of mine that found me through our common connections here on Instagram and just followed me.

I'd do well to quench my expectations and not think about David all the time now. Chances were he was doing something important that in no way, shape, or form was related to me.

I was thinking too much, thinking about things that were going to lead to my doom – and nothing more. And that was something I couldn't allow to happen at all. In terms of money-making, I was doing quite well now, and I needed to keep that up. I couldn't wait to pay Oisin all I owed.

But then, on a whim, I tapped the notification that had shown up, my heart skipping a beat once my eyes landed on what was happening here – and why I should stop thinking that our relationship was nothing more than his business pleasure.

David had just followed me on Instagram.

* * *

I'd never thought this would be happening one day. David, of all people, following me on Instagram? I did have some photos and followers, but I'd never thought... this had any chance of happening. And the fact he did it now meant he was online at this very moment, probably checking out all my photos.

Or maybe not. Perhaps all he was doing now was something else that didn't have any relation with the fact he was following me now.

Fuck. My heart was beating so fast a physician would probably think I was on the verge of having a heart attack. My hands felt a little clampy too, sweaty, and I had no idea what was going to happen now.

I was still in my house, alone, and hearing the sound of cars driving on the road in front of it. Sometimes I felt lonely, but never this lonely. I didn't like the look of this at all, though. Something seemed to be up, and I was going to find out what it was.

Well, I sure as hell wasn't going to continue doing nothing. The least I could do was to return the favor – follow him back, and hope my racing heart was going to calm down. This being the middle of the night, I was going to have to wake up tomorrow morning and get ready for classes and then work in the evening. I needed the rest.

I stopped when I thought better about what I was really doing here. Was all this worth it or was I doing this because I had a crush on the guy? That was the kind of thought I didn't want to prod much.

Didn't want to try to answer it at the time being.

I still tapped on the button and followed him. I waited to see if he was going to shoot me a message too and then tell me he'd been waiting for me to show up in his place or something like that.

Nothing more than the fruit of my wild imagination that was, though, I thought before cementing the fact that me and him together was never going to happen.

But then, all of sudden, there was another notification at the top of my screen. This time, it had to be something that didn't concern me at all – or just something that wasn't going to interest me.

Still, I tapped the notification and was brought right back to the DM part of the Instagram app. *It was David!* And he'd sent me a message. What he was hoping to talk with me right now, I didn't know, but I couldn't help but read his message nonetheless.

David: Hey, Renae. It's good to have found you here. Is this your professional profile?

My professional profile? For a moment I didn't know how to answer that question, but then it struck me that he'd been looking for me online because he'd been probably thinking he needed to set up a date with me or something like that.

That would be nice. However, it would be a little disappointing too. I'd been hoping he was going to tell me something-

Stop, Renae. You are only hurting yourself thinking that this guy cares about you in that way. He's rich and chances are he'd been looking for something more in his league – not a loser like you that has no right to think you can claim a man like him.

I sighed.

That part of my mind was right, as always.

Me: It's good to be talking to you as well. And... yeah, I think this is my professional profile.

David: You think, or are you sure?

Shit. I didn't start this on the right foot, did I? Now the man was most likely thinking he'd landed on the wrong profile and was being a bother to me. I needed to make sure he thought that wasn't the case.

Me: I'm sure. It's good to be talking to you. Wanna set up a date with me or something like that?

If we dated, then he would have even more reasons to come to the club tomorrow night. And then I'd milk the money out of him – as usual.

David: Sure thing. Would love to meet you right now.

My heart was beating like a galloping horse, the fact I was going to meet up with him tonight – a night where I was having insomnia problems – solidifying in my mind. I didn't know if I was doing the right thing or not, but sure as hell was going to follow through with it. There was nothing I'd rather be doing now, after all.

I killed the screen of the phone and began to dress appropriately for the meeting. Only my best clothes would do for this, and in no way, shape, or form could I disappoint him. He needed hostess me showing up at the restaurant he invited me to.

It took me a while, but I eventually found some pieces that made me feel okay with how I looked. Checking myself out in the mirror, all I could see was the look of a woman that was confident for this meeting.

Though... Now that I was thinking about it, a man like David would most likely appreciate it if I brought someone else for the meeting.

I shook my head at the thought of doing that, though. He could appreciate if I brought someone else in case the meeting with him didn't turn out to be what he was hoping it was going to be. Otherwise, we needed to be alone.

My mind was such a mess right now, but it didn't matter. It wasn't going to get in the way of me doing the right thing for David.

Chapter 6

I stopped in front of the building, my heart racing. I looked inside it, and there he was, already waiting for me. Though I couldn't be sure of it, he was making me think he was single and was doing this because he was thinking it would be nice if I became more than his hostess. Maybe like his girlfriend or something like that.

I killed that thought then and there. It would do me no good to be thinking that sort of thing right now.

I took a deep breath and walked into the building. The cold air of the AC snapped me right back from my reverie and to the reality that was beginning to settle in. David was here and he was doing this for me.

Or for him.

Whatever was the case, I needed to continue looking my absolute best for him. Nothing else would do.

I padded to him while hoping I wasn't looking like an idiot. I'd put on the right makeup and the correct amount of it. While I was not confident in myself at the moment – it had been a different feeling getting out of my home – I needed to make him think I was a hostess who was assured of herself.

If that didn't happen... I didn't want to think about what the consequences would be like. He'd probably ask the boss of Le Kissr to kick me out and go out of his way to never see me again.

There was a professionalism that needed to be followed in my line of work, and it wasn't the kind of thing I could just ignore.

I stood in front of him now, his eyes raking me over. I wore a skintight dress that showed the best of my curves – for him, only. My body was his at the moment, and any man willing to step through that boundary would have to face the harshest of consequences.

David was the possessive kind of man. He wouldn't like it if anyone – and especially another man – began to think he had any chance with me.

But of course, that would be after assuming he had the crush on me I was thinking he had. After all, for what other reason would he have requested me to come here as his hostess?

And coming here like that meant doing everything in my power to make sure he was going to have a good time.

"Hey there," I said, sitting down on a chair across from him.

I wondered if I was doing the right thing, sitting farther from him than he might be thinking I should. If he gave me any signs he would like me to sit closer to him, then I wouldn't object to doing it.

But right now... Right now I didn't fully know what his feelings for me were.

I cleared my throat, looking as uncomfortable as ever. I was making a fool of myself, and I knew that. Still didn't know if I was truly doing the right thing by having come here or if I should be excusing myself out as soon as possible.

The latter was the kind of thing I couldn't imagine myself doing. I wasn't going to do it. Not without his okay and if he was feeling like I was crossing a line here or doing something just as stupid. For the time being, all I could do was to continue breathing slowly.

His eyes seemed to penetrate me. Ocean blue, his gaze on me was making me feel like I was someone special – other than the person he thought of as nothing more than the hostess that tended to his every need.

His body was so muscular. David was such a hulking man he was making me feel like jumping right off this chair and hug him. I'd pull him for a tight hug – one that he would never be able to forget for the rest of his life.

His Adam's apple bobbed up and down. Was he feeling nervous too? My heart was beating like a speeding train in my chest. It was slamming against my ribcage, making me wonder if I was indeed doing the right thing.

He still hadn't said anything, and he kept looking at me with a gaze that told me a million things about myself, but none about the man that made so many of my nights hard to sleep.

I'd do anything just to have a proper night with him, one where I didn't have to pretend I was nothing more than his hostess. That's what he most likely thought of me, but I was still hopeful there was going to be a chance – anything that might make him realize he was missing out on a lot by not allowing me further into his life.

As usual, he wore a dark suit with a white tie. It made him look so huggable and kissable, the thought of bringing him into my home and then sleeping with him seeping into my mind. I was hoping so much that could happen one day, but then again, I didn't want to build expectations that couldn't be met.

He cleared his throat again and finally said, "Renae, it's good to see you here."

His eyes looked rather shifty, like he knew that by staring at me too much he was making me think he had a hidden feeling for me – something he thought he shouldn't share with me. The feeling of caring for him kicked in, and I shot my hand right up. The waiter came and we ordered some drinks.

For the time being, this was all it was going to be – nothing more than a night where he was going to feel pampered.

"You look beautiful tonight," he said, his voice a little throaty for my liking.

I didn't know if he was feeling nervous or not, but David certainly didn't look like his normal self. And that kind of bothered me a little. It told me I needed to act now instead of letting my inactivity ruin everything for me. It might not make me feel good, better about myself, but I knew it was the right thing to do.

And if that meant continuing this nerve-wracking small talk I was having with him, then so be it.

"And you look as handsome as always," I told him.

"How are you feeling tonight?"

"Okay, I guess."

His Adam's apple bobbed up and down. His hands kept wringing under the desk and part of me couldn't help but beg the waiter to come here soon rather than later with our drinks. I hadn't talked much yet, but my throat was already so dry. I needed to do something about that before my voice sounded like his.

And that was something I couldn't allow to happen.

"David... I don't know how to begin this..."

There it was. I was going to do the unimaginable, bringing up something he was most likely not thinking about right now. I was going to make a fool of myself, but it still felt right to be doing so. I didn't know what his reaction was going to be like, but he was still doing everything in his power to tell me I wasn't too wrong about an assumption that, one day, I'd thought would never be more than that.

"Begin... what?"

"I've been thinking about how much you care for me, and that is really sweet..."

I gave him the bait, but it didn't seem he was going to bite it. His eyes still looked at me with a ferocity mixed with nervousness I'd never seen before. It was clear as day this whole thing was making him feel uncomfortable, but still, if he was here, then he was okay with feeling that way.

I just needed to continue looking imponent, confident, even if those things didn't reflect my current emotions at all.

"And I was thinking I should know more about you. This whole time we've been meeting, and I still don't really know what your job is like..."

"I... run a company. I told you about it before, and it's one of the most important of its line of business. But I don't know why you want to learn about it..."

"It's because, without knowing that kind of information, I don't think I can continue treating you with the respect you deserve."

"What do you mean? You treat me like a King."

Ahhhh. I hadn't thought he was going to say that all of sudden, and now he was making me feel like screaming and asking for help. I had no idea how to go about this and find out what his feelings for me truly were. While I didn't want to admit this right now in front of him, I was falling in love with him. I was falling so much for him I was kind of thinking I wouldn't be able to live without him, if for some reason he disappeared from my life all of sudden.

But that wasn't going to happen, right? No way that would ever happen. I needed to focus on the good things at the moment. David was right here, with me, and he was making me feel like the stupidest girl in the whole district.

This Italian restaurant looked nice, the smell of pasta and lasagna and pizza wafting in the air, but that was still nothing compared to the man sitting in front of me. Looking as imponent as ever, and making me think that something other than me looking like a damn fool was going to come out of this.

I needed to do something about how this was going, and fast, or else he was going to think I was having a stroke or something like that. This conversation was making me feel too nervous, the thought of him–

Stop.

Renae, you really need to focus on what is happening right in front of you. Look at the signs. What are they telling you? Is he looking nervous? If he is, then you might have a chance.

Otherwise, you are just wasting your time.

My mind was right about that, and he did look uncomfortable. Looked more nervous than he should, which was surprising. He was a man of a different caliber. Most of the time, he didn't feel like this.

And so much was happening around us, and I couldn't focus on any of it. All I could focus on was the man sitting right in front of me, his eyes still making me feel like he wanted to ask me many questions, but didn't know how to go about doing that.

We had dinner and everything. He took me out to the back alley behind the restaurant, with nothing more than a single, warm bulb casting light into the premises. His eyes still looked at me like he had a lump in his throat.

But then, all of sudden, David pushed me against the wall. "Renae... I know this might sound a little too sudden, but I've been thinking about you for a long time. Ever since we first met in Le Kissr, in fact..."

Wait. Was he really telling me what I was thinking he was? Was he saying he'd been in love with me this whole time and that I'd been a fool not to have noticed it before? Fucking hell. I had no idea what was going on in his mind at the moment, but he was turning back into the confident man I'd met at the club.

If he'd been thinking those things about me this whole time, then I probably already lost the chance I had to correspond him with the same love. The same intensity of it. Chances were he was thinking I was never going to be anything more than his hostess.

Nothing more than the person he met when going for a cheaper hooker he couldn't touch.

* * *

His hot breath tickled my nose, his lips getting so close to touching mine. He put one hand on the wall behind me and then the other when I considered running away from here. His eyes were locked with mine, and I could tell he was thinking about doing something wrong with me. Something he might regret later on.

But that's the thing. Even if that came to pass, it wouldn't matter to him. I was nothing more than the hostess he fell in love with. And that was a feeling hard for him to control. His heart was beating so fast right now.

I put my hand on his chest, feeling the firmness of it. The heat of his body pulsed to me, making me feel like kissing his soft, plump lips right at this instant. I could almost read what was on his mind, but still decided not to do it.

He was more than willing to continue doing this with me, this tease, and I was eager to let him do it.

My pussy was getting wetter by the second, and all I could do was to listen to his next words.

"Tell me you want this. Tell me, or else I'm going to leave this place. And if that happens, I'll never come back."

"I want this," I murmured right back, telling him all he needed to know.

And like on cue, his lips met mine, sending a jolt of electricity through my body. My nipples hardened at the same instant. His body began to grind against mine, his hands pulling me to him and delivering so many powerful, hungry kisses I didn't know what to be feeling anymore.

All I could feel was how hungry he was for this, his hands now fumbling with my breasts right where someone could see and report us to the police. But with luck, that wasn't going to come to pass. And I couldn't care about that, either.

He was kissing me now. David was doing that and making me realize how stupid I'd been this whole time for not accepting the signs for what they were. He'd always been desperate for me. David never had a girlfriend, or a wife.

It wasn't long until I felt this was going to get out of control and that I needed to do something about it. I really, really didn't want anyone finding out about this, and where we were doing it was the perfect spot for that.

I put my hand on his chest and pushed him off me a little. His eyes gleamed with judgment when he spoke.

"You don't want this anymore?"

"No, it's just that," I said, chuckling, "someone could see us and I don't want to feel like I ruined your life or something like that."

"Oh, but it wouldn't ruin it. Not a chance in hell that would ever happen."

His eyes were like two globes that kept looking at me, kept making me feel like the most desired and precious woman in the world. And I continued to gaze at him as if he were the most important person on the planet.

And he just might be.

His hand found mine and I could tell he cared about me more than he should. His fingers brushing against mine, I had no choice but to kiss him again. In fact, I could kiss him right now as many times as I wished.

I knew he was enjoying it.

His body was like a moving wardrobe. He was so big, and I couldn't help but let out a gasp when he pulled me harder to him again.

"Don't know what is going on in that pretty little head of yours, but you are not leaving this place without sharing all your feelings with me. Renae, I need you so much."

And I knew he was telling me the truth. The more this went on, the more he told me those things, the more I fell in love with him. That was his plan, wasn't it? To make me fall in love with him so much I'd be wrapped around his finger.

He wouldn't let me leave, then.

His body was so enormous he made me feel small, and I wasn't one of the most petite women out there. His hands appeared to be everywhere too, pulling me to him, groping me, even going as far as pulling the chest cleavage of my dress down.

I locked my eyes with his and I could tell what he was thinking about right now. *Do I have your okay?* Hell yeah, he did.

He didn't need to ask for it twice.

David smiled and slid his hand underneath the chest cleavage of my dress. His fingers were so needy and hot as he groped my breasts in the alleyway some more. I looked to the side and then to the other, but didn't find anyone coming this way.

Thank fucking goodness we were alone.

What if Le Kissr found out about this? The thought worried me for a moment before realizing it wouldn't matter anyway. The club would just brush it off as something that simply happened in a hot meeting between the hostess and her client.

And this was the natural development, what would always have happened.

He lost his mind because of me and now couldn't stop thinking about me.

But out of nowhere, the sound of footsteps approached us. He pushed himself off me in the same instant and then cleared his throat. I missed his hand fumbling my breast and wished it would come right back, but there appeared to be something going on here we needed to tend to.

A short, rather fat woman showed up at the other end of the alleyway. It wasn't too long, so she couldn't be more than a couple of feet from us. And looking at that frame, that face...

Wait a minute. I know that person!

Chapter 7

I couldn't have forgotten those looks, the way she walked, and everything else about her even if I'd been trying to do that. She was rather short and a little on the chubby side, but she was the only person other than David here I cared about.

And her showing up here all of sudden. How the hell did it come to pass? What was she doing here?

"Renae? What are you doing here with that man?" She asked, sounding concerned.

I cleared my throat and dusted off the sides of my dress with my hands.

"Uuuhhhhh..."

I was unsure how to proceed with this, how to answer her. I didn't want to leave her hanging, though, so I guessed that something needed to be said. If she was here, then she was most likely worried David was a criminal trying to rob me or something like that.

I hoped she didn't call the police. But she could very well have already done that, considering the kind of person she was. There had been far too many times she surprised me with something she shouldn't have done.

"He's... a friend of mine," I answered.

"Just a friend?"

What kind of question was that now? No, he was much more than that to me, but I also wasn't going to tell her that. I'd been keeping the whole David thing locked behind many doors this whole time, finding it impossible to as much as mention to her I had a huge, hard crush on him.

"Yeah, just that," David said all of sudden, forcing me to shut my lips.

I was going to tell her that, but then I thought it was shitty of me to have been keeping this whole thing secret for so long. Kristin wasn't stupid. She knew something was up, and once she had enough time to process it, she was going to come right to me to tell me I should have been more open to her about it.

And believe me, I was feeling a little bad right now that I'd felt I couldn't trust her with that secret of mine. But then again, I'd also felt like I couldn't really figure the guy out – what his true thoughts for me were – and so I ended up not telling her anything.

That had been something that I alone could have figured out, and I was happy I waited this whole time until the final solution presented itself to me.

She walked through the shadow that was hiding her face and offered her hand to David, "It's nice to meet you. My name's Kristin."

"It's David, and it's good to know Renae has someone else looking out for her."

David's hand was shaking a little, but other than that, he didn't look too uncomfortable with how things were going. If anything, he was hoping we could resume what we were doing as soon as possible.

So that he could continue kissing me and making me feel like the best woman in the whole world.

"I know, right? This whole time she's been keeping so many things from me, and I don't think I even know her anymore."

She looked at me upon finishing saying those words. I couldn't help but feel a lump growing in my throat. So that's what she'd been thinking this whole time since I began to work as a hostess in Le Kissr.

Kristin didn't study with me in the same college class – in fact, we hadn't been seeing each other often since leaving high school – but I still didn't feel comfortable telling her about my job.

I didn't want to do that because I didn't want to listen to her words she would have had for me. *You are doing the wrong thing. You are killing yourself and it pains me to see you that way, Renae.*

She was a tough girl. I gave her that much.

David cleared his throat. "So, what are you doing here?"

"What are you doing here in the middle of an alley, kissing my friend?"

Oh shit. She saw everything and wasn't going to drop the matter until she squeezed everything out of it. I already knew that was going to happen, but I still had had some hope in my heart she would pretend that nothing of the sort was what transpired.

She could have been watching us making out since the beginning, wondering why the hell I hadn't told her anything about a new boyfriend of mine.

David looked at me, unsure of how to proceed with this. To win against Kristin, he was going to need my help. No way around that.

I stepped to her and said, "He had a sauce stain on his shirt I was trying to clean. Nothing more than that."

"Nothing more than that, really? You think I'm going to believe something like that?"

Then and there I realized that continuing to lie to her was going to do me no good, so I grabbed her hand and said to David, "We just need to talk, in private."

"I'm going to be here, waiting," he said.

His words warmed my heart. I'd thought he was going to leave. I was so glad he didn't.

"Kristin... David and I have been meeting recently..."

"He's your new boyfriend? Why didn't you tell me anything about that before?"

"It's a bit complicated. I didn't want to tell you anything because I didn't know what his feelings for me were."

"Well, you could have let me help you out with that."

I sighed. "I guess so, and there's one more thing about me I need to tell you."

"What kind of thing?"

"I've been working as a hostess, in Le Kissr."

She covered her mouth in an instant, her action telling me all I needed to know. She couldn't believe I'd been keeping something like that secret from her this whole time. To be honest, I couldn't believe as well I'd been doing that. I liked Kristin a lot, but I'd still thought it wouldn't have been a good thing if she'd learned about it from the get-go.

"Why did you start working there?"

I exhaled, looking at David as I hoped he could just come right here and answer all of her questions instead. I knew he would be able to do it. David knew so much about me now.

"Because I needed the money. I loaned some more money from Oisin, and working there was the only way I had to make enough to pay him up."

"Jesus fuck, I hadn't thought that things were that bad for you. You should still have told me about it. I might have been able to help you out with something."

That was a nice thought and all, but I doubted she would have been able to do it. Kristin didn't have that kind of pull, and she couldn't have made it so the bank would have let me borrow the money from them instead.

Borrowing money from a bank would have been better, sure, but I didn't have a good financial history. Too many debts still to be paid. In fact, my financial history was so bad it was a wonder Oisin decided to lend me that money. I'd thought he was just going to say for me to fuck off.

"I know, and it's bad. David really isn't just my friend. We were kissing, and you saw everything."

"I did, and I have to say, he's pretty hot."

I looked into her eyes, unsure how to proceed with this.

"Still... I don't know if dating him is the right thing to do. My ex... I don't want to think about him, but he kidnapped me not too long ago, and I'm not sure I'm ready to face that kind of thing again, if it comes to pass. I doubt David would ever do something similar, but that's the thing. I can't be sure of that until it happens or not."

Kristin smiled.

"I don't think you have to worry about that, and I'm glad at least you told me about the kidnapping."

"Yeah, at the time I needed to vent about it to someone. I'm glad you are not mad I'd been keeping this whole thing secret for so long."

"Oh, but I'm mad about it," she joked, opening another wide smile. "And yet, I can't do anything about it, can I? Getting mad at you now won't help anyone, and I know you need my help and support now more than anything."

I admired how she was reacting to all this. I'd thought she was going to tell me I was in the wrong for having kept her in the dark, but she was being a good sport about it. She was making me feel a little bad about it, though. Kristin was someone I could have trusted with my secrets from the beginning.

"Well, now that everything is out of the way, how about having dinner with us?" Kristin offered.

I wouldn't call it dinner, but okay. We could eat something else in the restaurant. This was going to be another night I wasn't going to be able to sleep well, but that was okay. Not much I could do about that.

We entered the restaurant and had a good time in it. When walking out of it, Kristin said, "You two look like two cute little love birds. Don't be shy about it! You can kiss in front of me. After all, it wouldn't be the first time."

I looked at him and couldn't help but do it as she suggested we should do, sealing my lips with his and feeling like the happiest woman in town. His lips were so plump, so ready for kissing. We must have kissed each other for minutes, for even Kristin cleared her throat so that it would end.

I pulled myself off him a little, but was still close enough to feel the odor of his cologne penetrating my nostrils. I felt like kissing him again and again, multiple times. It was such a pity this was ending and I wasn't going to be able to do that, I thought while shifting my weight to my other foot.

"Now that I know what is really happening here, what you are doing when I'm not looking," Kristin said, approaching me with a wide smile on her face. "I can finally help you, and don't worry, I'm not going to tell anyone about this."

"Thank you, Kristin. Knew I could count on you.'

"You can always count on me. I would never let you down," she said after turning and getting inside her car. She pulled out and took another road, disappearing when she rounded the block.

The cold air of the night kissed my face, and I couldn't help but feel like kissing him again. I knew he was more than willing, his eyes telling me all I needed to know. And so, without delaying it any further, I pulled him to me.

Our lips connected, and I could tell he needed to stop this and say something to me. Something he'd thought he would never mention in his life again.

"Renae, I love you."

I looked into his eyes. Love and care filled them. He meant those words, and he wasn't going to leave this place if I didn't retribute the love he'd been seeking this whole time. His words made my heart melt, and I couldn't help but tell him exactly what he'd been waiting to come out of my lips.

"I love you too, David."

And so, having said that to him, everything changed, and our lives were very different since then.

* * *

I was walking on the sidewalk when my eyes landed on him. Not on David. He couldn't be here, after all. It was someone else. A man I'd presumed I'd never meet again in my life.

My ex. Troy, and he had a smug smirk on his face. He knew he'd gotten me where he needed me and that short of someone stopping to figure out what was going on here, nothing was going to stand in his way.

His way of getting revenge for the fact I managed to put him in jail.

"Renae, it's good to see you here."

We were in the middle of downtown. If I screamed, someone would step in. I should feel safe, but couldn't. It was like something was squeezing my heart, making me feel as if I was going to have a stroke or something like that.

His eyes seemed to penetrate me now, looking at me not like the former girlfriend he'd once had, but like a cockroach he should stomp as soon as possible.

Even though there were a multitude of people walking around us, hurrying over to their destinations , I felt like I was alone.

Those faceless people didn't make me feel safer. They made me sure I was going to have to deal with him on my own, and it appeared that was going to be the case.

"Troy... I don't know what you are thinking you are doing, but we have nothing else to talk about."

He lifted his right arm, impeding me from rushing away from him as fast as my legs could take me. He lowered it then, his eyes softening up.

"I didn't come here to kidnap you again if that's what you are thinking," he said, smiling.

The fucker still thought that had been nothing more than him loving me too much, or something like that. That's what his lawyer told the judge, and he sucked it up, lowering the number of years he had to spend in jail. Lowering them to a couple of months only, and now he was out. Out and ready to do whatever he was considering doing with me.

I hadn't thought about him this whole time. Could it be he'd been tailing me this whole time, just waiting for the right opportunity to talk to me?

I shifted my weight and said, "I don't want to see you ever again. Get away from me."

My heart rate was quickening. I needed to calm myself down. Being nervous in front of him was going to do me no good.

I calmed down my racing heart, focusing on it while my eyes examined the man in front of me. He'd come here to tell me something important, and I needed to find out what that was.

"Troy... What the hell do you think you are doing here now?"

"I need to tell you something about David."

So, he finally found out what his name was. Figured he should know, considering David pressed charges against him too after the kidnapping. I wondered what his life was going to be like from now on. Was he finally going to see the error of his ways and focus on getting a good job, maybe even turn things around for him?

I doubted that was going to happen. He wasn't that kind of man. He didn't want to let it come out, but what happened hurt his heart. He was never going to recover from it – not as the same man anyway.

Still, what did he need to tell me about David anyway that I didn't already know? I studied his eyes, hoping to find the answer to that, but he was a harder man to read this time. Seriousness filled his eyes. It was clear as day this meeting meant a lot to him.

I wasn't about to pardon him for all the things he did, but still... I could tell that prison time did well for him. He got out of there as a different man.

"What do you know about him?" I asked.

"He's not the person you are thinking he is."

"Is that so?"

He nodded. "He's hiding his true identity from you. The guy that hired me to abduct him still wants him, and he has his reasons for that."

This was making me feel uncomfortable now. I didn't think David had been doing something wrong, but the way my ex was telling me those things... It was almost as if he cared about me now and was doing all he could to keep me safe from my love.

Could it really be he'd been hiding something from me this whole time I should know about? David... I thought you and I already knew all we needed to know about each other. We made our relationship official. Everyone knew about it, and now you were more than my customer, but still... Troy was making me think he was right, that you've been hiding something from me I should know about.

I tipped my chin up. "You are not going to change my mind about him."

He sighed. "Maybe I can't change your mind, but you should know he's hiding something. He's knee-deep in some shit not even I thought he was, and that is saying something, considering it's coming from me."

He approached me, pedestrians around us still heading to their destinations. Someone should have already seen he was making me feel uncomfortable and done something about it, but none appeared ready to do it.

I felt alone once again, despite the number of all kinds of people that surrounded us.

Troy towered over me as he spoke, "Look, I don't want to make you think I'm worth you or something like that right now, but you should ask him about his... other life, the one he doesn't show you when you are not looking."

And gazing into his eyes, I could tell he really cared about me. Troy cared about this, and he couldn't help but hope I was going to heed his words. Problem was, doing that was easier said than done – much, much so.

He breathed in and then out. "I'm not going to do anything right now you don't like, and I'm leaving already. Just be careful around him."

And having said that, he turned and left, disappearing among the crowd of people that surrounded us. I stood there like an idiot, not knowing how to be feeling about this. Should I heed his words to find out if he was right or not?

Most of all, I didn't want to think there was something vile behind David he hadn't been telling me about.

He was the perfect man for me. Why should I care about that sort of thing?

The thought of him hiding something worried me. Troy wouldn't have done what he did if it didn't have an ounce of truth in it.

Maybe I need to pay more attention to what David does from now on.

Chapter 8

I was with him, in our bedroom. His bedroom, to be more precise. With him and having the time of my life. We were all alone here. We couldn't even hear the sound of cars and motorcycles driving on the street below. His apartment was just so big it filled a whole floor. His bathroom was the kind of thing I would never forget. It'd been a long time since I last shared a bathroom with a man.

His hand looked for mine. Holding it, he told me all I needed to know. He was going to keep me safe, loved, and cared for. His fingers brushed against mine, letting me feel how callous his hand was. It showed he was a man that worked hard in his life before finding himself where he was at the moment. David was a man that knew hardship.

I could feel the kind of love he felt for me. Of the kind that told me it was never going to fade. He was going to love me for the rest of his life. That was something he would never be able to deny.

His eyes looked for mine. I could tell how much tonight meant to him, though there were a couple of things that happened since he declared his love for me that got me thinking.

What his life was like when nobody was looking. But that was something that shouldn't worry me... Right? Troy told me what he thought I needed to know.

What he thought that should make me think twice about the kind of man he was. Who David was. But Troy was nothing more than an asshole. He didn't care about me. He didn't even care that once I loved him. He didn't care about any of those things.

All he cared about was making me feel miserable.

David's eyes met mine and I couldn't help but lean over for another powerful kiss. His lips felt so smooth, so needy, and it wasn't long until our kiss became a full-on smooch I was never going to forget.

His hand looked for my ass, which he squeezed. I gasped and pushed myself a little closer to him. I needed to feel him. Needed to feel his hard, pulsing prick pressing against my pussy.

No matter what happened here, I wasn't going to allow rumors about secrets of his life to ruin me. They weren't going to get in the way of our love.

His prick was so hard right now, as if it was thinking about getting inside me. Leading its way inside my waiting, throbbing pussy. And I was more than willing to let that happen. I knew it could and that it would make all the difference in the world for me.

I imagined him cumming inside me and then having tiny little babies we would love for the rest of our lives. That would be so great. So, so fucking great.

I looped my fingers around his hardness and wasn't surprised when it twitched. He was so close now. So close to cumming and making the aforementioned babies that my mind just couldn't stop thinking about.

This shouldn't take too long, I thought when I began to pump him. It wasn't just his dick I was feeling, how warm it was, but also the ruggedness of his ballsack.

It was hot, needy, and it was making me feel like taking it inside me too. I could just imagine the kind of thing I'd feel if he managed to bury his balls inside me. It would make me feel so fucking happy.

It would complete me like nothing before it ever did.

"Fuck, Renae. You are looking so hot today," he purred against my ear.

It was dark outside, but there was a lamppost just outside the window. Its light was sneaking through the blinds, showing how shy it was of inundating the whole room with its brightness.

I had a good night's sleep. I couldn't even remember when it was the last time I felt so safe and had a bad night. This was really like nothing else.

The more this went on, the more I felt like keeping this going on and on forever.

His cock ground against me. "Jesus, David. You are going to hurt me."

"Do you feel okay with that? Or is it bad if I hurt you right now?"

"No, it's fine. I need it. I need you hurting me. Make me feel pain."

He smiled. "That I can do, and so much more too."

"Yes, please. As much pain as needed. All of it."

His cock was eased in. He penetrated me, pushing himself hilt-deep. My pussy walls got stretched to their absolute limits. I felt like I was a virgin all over again and he was my first time. My first man. I couldn't believe I hadn't fallen in love before. Ever since Troy...

Fuck Troy.

All he cared about was making me feel miserable.

He got in all the way, now thrusting in and out with all his might. His hands kept me pinned against his muscular body. His sweat tickled my skin. I could feel how slick his body was.

And despite all the warmth, pain, and suffering he was making me feel, I was jubilant. I was overjoyed by all the things happening here.

His cock kept pulsing, thrusting in and out, and then stretching me to my absolute limits. All I cared about now was him cumming inside me.

He didn't have anything on. No protection. Nothing of the sort. He was doing this the raw way and he kept doing it with so much vigor I thought it was never going to end.

His balls caressed and slapped against my pussy lips. I moaned and squealed when he finally erupted inside me, filling me to the brim with all his milk.

There was so much of it that it began to leak out. I closed my legs tightly. I wasn't going to allow any more of it to come out. I needed all of his seeds inside me. All of it and nothing else. I was just that greedy.

His fingers brushed across my cheeks, his mouth opening to ask me something important. Something that couldn't be delayed any longer.

"Are you on your pill?"

I shook my head. No point in lying to him. I needed his babies so fucking much. Feeling one of them in my arms... It was something that would make my life feel complete, full. I hoped I was going to have many of them, even though I couldn't know that for sure right now.

I closed my eyes and fell asleep. I was dreaming about what our life was going to be like from now on when the sound of someone talking woke me up. I fluttered my eyes open and spotted David sitting on the other side of the bed, talking to someone.

His phone was glued to his ear, and even though his back was turned to me, his shoulders looked tense. Whatever it was he was talking about with that person, it seemed to be pretty important.

And I wished he would tell me about it.

"Yes, oh... he died?"

Who died? I wished I could find out about that, but didn't want to interrupt him. Then the memory of Troy mentioning he was a wolf hiding in the skin of a sheep struck me, almost making me sit right up.

If he was hiding something from me, then this was going to be the right time to lure that out into the open. I breathed in and out, trying to control my thoughts. It would do me no good to be nervous during a moment like this one.

I needed to be calm, or else he was going to notice I was overhearing him. He was probably thinking I was sleeping...

"Shit. I guess I'll need to go there and do something about it."

Do something about what? Whatever it was he was talking about, I needed to know. I kept my ears trained to whatever he was going to mention next.

"No, I don't think it's anything you need to worry about right now. He's dead and that's that. It's all going to pass."

Fucking dammit. He wasn't going to mention anything more relevant than what he already did, was he? He was going to keep talking in circles, mentioning things that didn't make any sense to me.

But one thing at least *did* make sense to me. He was hiding something important from me – something I needed to know and find out about.

I calmed my racing heart down. I still didn't know the full extent of his lies to me, but something needed to be done about them. I needed to do something about that before shit hit the fan.

He stood up from the bed and walked to the balcony. David looked as handsome as ever, making my heart feel like making me get off the bed right away and rush over to him. I needed to kiss him.

I just couldn't do it right now, though. The fact I was having to keep this hidden from him hurt me a little, but there wasn't much about that I could do right now. Between not telling him what I was thinking, what I was doing at the moment, and letting his lies ruin my love for him, the choice was pretty clear to my mind.

"Huh. Okay, yeah. It's just like I said. I'm going there to solve the issue before it's too late. Don't worry, it's not going to take me long."

He did mention something about someone dying and that being something that made him happy. He'd told me many times before he was nothing more than a businessman. I knew that overhearing his private phone talk was wrong, but as he put on his shirt and finished getting dressed, I couldn't imagine myself doing anything different.

I had a plan now, and it was going to come to fruition. Of that, I was sure.

I closed my eyes, but I could still feel as if he was looking at me. He was probably trying to find out if I'd get up anytime soon. But that wasn't going to happen. I was going to continue pretending I was having some of the best dreams of my life.

He closed the door and I sat up on the bed. I could hear the sound of his footsteps as he went to the elevator. I wasn't going to be able to take it when following him, so I was going to have to be a little smarter about this.

The stairs.

I got dressed as fast as possible and headed out of the room. Going to the door, I opened it and rushed down the stairs. I had no idea what awaited me at the end of this, but I believed I was doing this for the right reasons.

No matter what happened, I was going to stand by his side. I just needed to find out what side that was, and then I would tell him all he needed to know. I'd tell him again he was the love of my life.

I'd tell him that as many times as possible.

* * *

I took a taxi to follow him to this place. An old, forgotten apartment building on the outskirts of the town. The driver grumbled about something, but I wasn't able to make it out. I think he mentioned something about this part of the city being too dangerous to be driving around at this time of the night.

And he also said something about not liking having to tail other people.

He asked me about why I was doing this, but I just dodged the question. At the end of the day, he was nothing more than the driver, and it didn't matter to me at all if he cared about my wellbeing or not.

I came here with a mission in mind, and I was going to see it through.

He didn't mention anything else as he took off, driving slowly like I'd asked of him – and had to pay him more so that he would do it. Relief washed over me when I noticed this was going well. David wasn't going to find out I was here.

And he was probably thinking at the moment I was still sleeping in his bedroom, like a little angel he needed to keep safe at all times.

The neighborhood we were in was quite silent, and I couldn't see many houses with their lights still on. It took him quite a while to get here, and for what purpose... that I was soon going to figure out.

There was nothing he could keep hidden from me forever.

The night's light washed over me, and I couldn't help but feel a line of fear running up my spine when looking at the building in front of me. I gazed at it in wonder, thinking that something pretty bad had to be happening at the moment if he'd come here.

If he'd come here to be doing this, then... I didn't know what he was doing here – yet. He'd come here to solve some kind of issue.

I hugged myself and headed to the building. The front door was closed, so I tried the one at the back. Also closed. Spotting a window whose glass panel had been broken, I tried to propel myself into the building, but it was to no avail.

This wasn't going to work like that. It wasn't going to be that easy.

I turned my head to the side and spotted a ladder. Grabbing it, I took it to where I'd found that window. Now *this* is going to work. I climbed it and then jumped when I thought it was safe and that nobody would hear me doing this.

I perked up my ears, trying to hear if anyone was going to come this way. But no one was coming. I was all alone on the first floor of this building. That relieved me, but it didn't last very long. There was still a mission – something important that needed to be done here.

Finding out what it was that he'd been hiding from me this whole time.

I headed to the middle part of the living room, where I found a circular staircase that led to the second floor and to all the others. One step at a time, I reached the second floor, where then a noise startled me.

I almost gave away my position, my hand covering my mouth in a heartbeat. Thank goodness my reactions were still sharp, I thought to myself when I took a peek at what awaited me beyond here.

There was a guy with an assault rifle in his hands that appeared to be patrolling the second floor. He was going from here to there, more often than not stopping to survey the region with his eyes.

His eyes were half-closed. Looking rather boring, I couldn't help but think this was the right opportunity I'd been looking for. The one where I was going to get to the third floor.

And the third floor... I could already hear the sound of something coming from it. Grunts and groans. I had no idea what was going on here but, again, I was going to find out.

Nothing was going to stop me from doing that.

The guy headed to the other side of the floor. The room was quite dark, and he wouldn't be able to hear me. One good thing about being a girl was that I could get from place to place without making too much foot noise.

I snuck back to the staircase and then forced myself to the third floor. Looking down below, I couldn't hear or see anything that could tell me that guy from the second floor had heard something and was now rushing to me, ending my plans before they came to fruition.

I took a deep breath and headed to the fourth floor of the building. There were a couple of guys on the third floor too, but they were inside a room not doing anything special. Cracking open some beers and drinking and laughing. That sort of thing.

I managed to sneak into the fourth floor and found a semi-open open, light sneaking through the gap. I thought about not doing this, not continuing this, but knew that wouldn't be the right thing to do.

Now that I was here, I needed to see this through, no matter the cost.

David had already done far too many suspicious things. He'd come here in the middle of the night, didn't think he needed to leave a note telling me he would come back soon or something like that, and was in an old building that looked too shady for its own good.

What it was still doing here, and what it was used for, I didn't know, but I was going to find the answers soon enough.

I proceeded to the semi-open door on my toes, getting to it in less than about ten seconds. I could still hear the noises and the sounds coming from within the place. Whatever was going on here, it appeared to be pretty serious.

It made me feel nervous.

I stopped when I got to the door, my ears still hearing everything. Sounds of punches, kicks, and the like filled the atmosphere. I could also hear the sound of the guys from the third floor laughing as they watched their European soccer game. What they were doing didn't matter to me at all, but their presence made me remember that whatever happened here now, I was going to be all alone if David disapproved of this, of what I was doing.

I didn't want to think too much about what would then happen, and so I just peeked my head through the gap of the door.

My heart was beating like a speeding train, but I was still not afraid enough to just turn and run from here as fast as possible. I wasn't going to do that. I wasn't that stupid. Now that I was here, on this floor, there was only one path to choose from.

Just one choice to make.

And what I saw inside the room made my heart jump. David was here alright, but he wasn't alone. He was with some men that looked like the textbook definition of goons. Mean looking, bulging muscles, grease-smeared faces, and guns in their hands. High-quality guns at that, I noticed.

I almost let a gasp escape through my lips, covering my mouth. I was so relieved. I'd thought my cover was going to be blown.

Seeing David here with these men made my heart feel as if vines were squeezing it dry of the love I felt for him. I still loved him and thought that was never going to change, but still... What type of man was he really?

I needed to know the answer to that right away.

The guy that was getting the beating of his life was none other than... *Troy himself!* I almost couldn't believe what my eyes were seeing. This had to be some sort of joke, right? This couldn't be happening.

Why the hell was this happening to me now?

A tear rolled down my cheek, and that was when I made the last mistake of my life. I took a step into the room, but I didn't do it because I was thinking I needed to present myself to them, but because I just needed to shift my weight.

That's right. Just shifting my weight and do nothing more than that. But it became a costly mistake.

Their heads turned to me in a heartbeat, eyes narrowing. They never thought a woman would just show up all of sudden in their hideout, looking confused while disappointment clouded her face. My face.

David's eyes shot wide when he noticed it was me, of all people he thought I could be, the one standing right at the doorway.

"What the fuck are you doing here?" he asked all of sudden, rushing right to me.

His hand opened, grabbing my right arm. He pulled me into the room and closed the door. I didn't know what was making me feel worse about all this, if it was the fact he'd been hiding this side of his life from me this whole time, or that he kidnapped Troy, putting himself in the same position his assailant had been not too long ago.

"David. I came here because Troy told me you were hiding something from me."

His eyes surveyed me, assessing if I was telling him the truth or not. Even though he trusted me before with his life, he couldn't bring himself to share those same feelings. A lot had changed since then. A lot changed the moment he sniffed me out.

This forgotten, decaying building whose tint had long flaked off. This was all so stupid. It shouldn't be happening like this. David should be in his bedroom now, kissing me and telling me I was the love of his life.

"So, you don't trust me anymore," he murmured...

"No. That's not what I thought this was. He told me you were hiding something from me, and it turned out he was right."

He shook his head. "Still... doing this. I thought you were beyond it. I thought you trusted me, especially after having busted my ass off to save you from him."

"I'm thankful for everything you've done for me, but this... this is the kind of thing I can't ignore or excuse."

He shook his head and paced away from me. Troy was still sitting on the chair, tied with ropes to it. His face had blood smeared all over it, and there were cuts and concussions too. His eyes didn't look at me, and I feared he wasn't even conscious right now.

He still saw me coming in, though. He knew I was here. I didn't like him at all, but if there was one thing to appreciate about him, it was the fact he'd warned me about David.

David turned on his heels and barked, "I thought you really loved me! I've been doing this whole thing for you and no one else, but it seems it's nothing more than a waste of time. You think I was working behind your back or something like that."

"That's not what I was thinking you were doing. I didn't even know what I was going to find here."

"That still changes nothing. You could have talked to me face to face first. I would have told you about what I was doing."

"And what do you? Do you kidnap people for a living or something like that?"

"No... This has nothing to do with my job. I've been looking for this asshole since he kidnapped you. The police did nothing – as usual – and now I'm fixing that."

He grabbed a hammer and proceeded to Troy. I thought he was going to strike him with it, so I jumped ahead and stood in his way. I wasn't going to allow him to do something stupid like that right in front of me. No way I would have allowed that to happen.

I lifted my arms on either side of me and said, "I'm not going to stand and just watch you doing this. This is not who I thought you were." I paused, studying his eyes, and then added, "Are you trying to get some information out of him or something like that?"

"Look, I don't think I need to explain myself..."

His words hurt me. This whole time I'd been thinking he really cared about me, but now... Now he was looking at me with cold eyes. Eyes that told me he was going to get this thing done and that it didn't matter to him at all what I thought about it.

How I felt about this.

His business was more important to him than how he was making me feel. I felt my world falling apart at such a realization.

But I was still not going to let this continue. Doing this to Troy wasn't right. He kidnapped me, sure, but at least he didn't beat me up. He could have done that, but he didn't.

"David... I think it's over between us."

"I think the same, Renae. I did so many things for you, even getting this guy... only to have you betray me anyway. That sort of thing is inexcusable..."

"What is inexcusable is you not telling me at all what it is that you really do. How you really make money."

"Alright," he said, putting the hammer down on a small table and pacing in front of me. "You want to know about that? Fine. Then, I'm going to tell you all about it. Just don't act surprised, or cry."

"I'm not going to cry. I'm just... disappointed, and sad."

He cleared his throat. "Do you really want to know what my job is?"

I nodded. "Yes, I do."

"Then, I'm going to explain it to you," he said while all of his men in the room shifted their weights, some from the other floors finally coming here to find out what was happening. Their eyes widened when they spotted me. Some of them probably knew who I was, but they couldn't hide their disappointment in themselves. They were so carefree they didn't notice me coming in, and that was a mistake David here wasn't going to forgive.

"Boss, do you need us to deal with her?"

"No. I'm going to deal with you later."

The big guy with the goatee that asked that cleared his throat. He knew he'd fucked up. He was the guy that was on the second floor of this building. He looked so tired back then and was probably thinking not much was going to happen tonight. How wrong he turned about to be.

Poor man.

But worrying about what his future here was going to be like wasn't something that concerned me, and so I pushed that thought back to the depths of my mind. David turned his head to me. He was going to tell me what he really did behind the scenes, what his job was truly like, and I needed to hear each and every word that was going to come out of his mouth with the utmost attention.

I couldn't miss a single one.

"First, I think I need to say I'm sorry I got you mixed up in all this shit," he said.

I didn't know what to tell him. He was saying he was sorry... about that? A bit too late for it, but if he was really feeling that way, then it could be a step in the right direction. Still, I wasn't going to hold my breath to that.

He blinked and continued, "Alright. Guess we really are going to do this. I do run LifeSolutions. It's a company that works for me and I make a lot of money from it, but... that is not everything. I also operate a protection money operation in the district where you work, Renae. People there don't like me, but they've got no choice. They either pay for my protection, or The Ravagers will come to get everything they own. And that is not something they can afford to let happen. I'm their only option."

"So, it's extortion."

There was a twitch under his eye. "It's not that. They accepted the terms, and for the most part, they've all been paying well. There are some troublemakers, sure, but we deal with them."

"Deal with them? How?"

He chuckled. "I don't think you want to know that."

His expression was resolute, and it didn't seem this was affecting him much. But there was something in his eyes that was telling me a rather different story. Something he didn't want to share with me. I needed to find out what that was.

If there was a chance he could change his mind about this and see the light – the truth – then I needed to double down on it.

I needed to clear everything up here – no stone was going to be left unturned.

David marched to me. I didn't fear him, though. I knew there was no point fearing him. He wasn't going to beat me up or do something like that. But after this... I doubted he was going to let me walk out of here scot-free.

Maybe he was going to lock me up somewhere... I didn't know what was going to happen, but I still didn't like the direction this was taking. I needed to be on my toes all the time here. It was the only way to make sure the worst wasn't going to occur.

"Do you want to know how Troy came to be here?"

I crossed my arms over my chest. "You kidnapped him. What's there to know about that?"

"Well, I didn't do that just because he's an asshole that abducted you. I did it because he has information on The Ravagers we need, and he isn't going to leave this building until he tells me all he can about them."

"He isn't even awake anymore. I think you might have killed him, asshole."

I couldn't believe I just called David that, and it did make something under his left eye twitch. Maybe this was really affecting him in more ways than I thought possible, but for now I wasn't going to make any assumptions.

They weren't worth it.

David chuckled, grabbed his hammer again, and then struck Troy with it on his belly, making him gasp as he shot his eyes wide. They beat him up so badly I'd assumed he was unconscious before the hit, and that made me feel sorry for him. Sorry for him while my blood boiled at the thought I'd once loved David.

Heat was bubbling up inside my heart. I couldn't believe this. I couldn't believe this was happening. I'd thought David was a good man.

"See? I told you he was awake."

"Nothing of that changes anything."

He shook his head. "Renae. You are nothing more than a hostess. Go back to your job and forget about this."

Wait. He was actually going to allow me to do that? He was going to allow me out of here? Was that for real, or nothing more than a trap?

I should have told Kristin about this. She would have called the police. But when I was coming here, the thought didn't even cross my mind. And even if it had, I wouldn't have thought it was the right thing to do.

Calling the police on the guy that promised his love to me? That was not something I would be okay with. I wouldn't have been okay with it.

"And you are... just going to let me walk out? Just like that?"

"Sure, why not? It's not like you really have any proof on what is going here. And ah, just to be sure of that, I'm going to have to frisk you."

I thought he was going to ask one of his goons to do it, but it was him who padded to me. David stopped in front of me, his eyes raking me over. I could tell that something different was going on in his eyes, but I couldn't pinpoint the origin of it – what it truly was.

His hands went for my legs, and then he moved them up. He checked out my pockets, my groin region, breasts – everything. With him, a stone was never left unturned. I did bring my phone for this, but I didn't remember to use it.

Now that I was thinking about it, it would have been good to make use of it to record all the things he'd said. It would still have led to nothing, since he would have found out about it and destroyed the recording, but... I should have been smarter about this.

I was so stupid for not thinking I was going up against David by coming here, and not simply spying on him. Everything would be fine now, though.

"So, what is going to happen now?" I asked before tipping my chin up. He wasn't going to make me afraid of him. No chance that would ever happen.

"I'm going to make the mistake of letting you out and then... I don't want to see you ever again. The thing you did, coming here and then sneaking into the building. I can't love a woman that doesn't trust me."

"I'd argue it was you who didn't trust me first. I told you about Troy. I told you all about him. I think I deserve... Forget it. I'm just going to leave."

He grabbed my arms, his nails digging deep into my skin.

"And don't you dare to call the police on me. I'll be watching. I'll have someone watching you all the time until I'm sure you are not going to be a problem."

I shook my arm until it was free. "Don't worry about that. I don't think the police would be able to do anything anyway."

And I couldn't believe the direction this was taking. I'd spent so much time with him and he'd bought me so many gifts. But they'd been all for nothing. Everything we did was for nothing. Our time spent together didn't mean anything to him anymore.

His eyes looked rather cold as he stared me down, gesturing with his head for his men to lead me out of the building.

I peeked over my shoulder and thought of Troy. He was an asshole still, but he was the prelude to everything that ended up happening. Why did I think that trusting another man was an okay thing to do?

All I could now was to hope that my life was going to turn around for the best.

Chapter 9

I opened the door, stepping into her room. I was so glad she let me come here. Live here for the time being. I told Kristin people were going to be watching me all the time, and she said it didn't bother her.

She was such a good friend I couldn't believe I really had her still. I lost so many friends growing up. It turned out they were not my friends after all.

Her room showed a little bit of her personality. The walls were painted a soft tone of purple and her couch was one the best things ever. I'd been here a couple of times before and I swear her couch was better for sleeping than her bed.

There were mood lights all over in the living room and I could sniff the smell of something delicious wafting in the air. She was baking a cake? Wonderful! That was the sort of thing I needed to clear up my head.

She bounced to me, coming from the other end of the living room, her arms stretched out wide. She hugged me and buried her head in my shoulders. Kristin was short, but fat.

She hugged me with enough strength to make air leave my lungs. I patted her on her back and said, "Thank you, Kristin, for letting me stay here for a little while."

She moved away from me as relief washed over me. "It's okay. I know you need the help, and I'm here for that. No way I'd ever allow anyone to hurt you."

Her eyes glistened with her love and care for me. Wished I could become a lesbian so that we could be more than friends. She loved me so much. Kristin was part of the family I never had.

"Thank you again. Is that cake you are baking?"

"Oh, yes it is," she responded before making a beeline to the kitchen. I followed her. The light of the morning sun was sneaking through the blinds of her window.

This was such a fine morning, and I couldn't help but feel like spending the rest of my life here. Living here together with her would be nice, but then again, I didn't want to cause her any more trouble than I already was.

The table was ready. We had our slices of chocolate cake on dishes and Kristin was sitting across from me. She was eating her cake like it was the most delicious thing in the world – and it sure as hell might be.

"So... it turned out he's nothing more than a criminal in disguise, right?" She asked, holding a rather dirty spoon in her hand.

I shook my head, letting my shoulders drop. "I never once thought he was..."

"Well, the good thing is that you won't have to see him ever again. The thing he did to Troy... you need to do something about it. Call the police on his ass."

"Yes, but they have someone watching me. Watching us. I'm pretty he's s already outside. It's just that we can't see him."

"You are probably right about that, but still... I'm not worried. I'm not afraid, and you should be as well."

"How am I not going to be when he told me the kind of person he is? He could kill me now and nothing would happen against him. No one would try to jail him if they found out he did it."

"Don't let it intimidate you. I'm sure you can come up with something to put him back in his place."

I chewed down another piece of the slice of the cake I was eating.

"Thank you, but I'm not sure I can do that."

"Why not?" Her eyes penetrated me as she looked at me, trying to find out what I was truly thinking.

"Because..." I pushed the cake in my throat down. "I think I still love him."

She spewed the cake she was munching.

"What? You are pulling my leg here, right? Please tell me you are."

"I know it's not normal, but still. I can't deny the fact that everything about him makes me want to be with him again..."

I stood up from the chair I was sitting on and walked to the window. Looking outside, I couldn't see anyone suspicious. There didn't appear to be anyone keeping an eye on the place, but I was still pretty sure someone was doing that.

I could feel as if someone was standing right behind me, hand on my neck and...

I needed to forget David. Thinking about him now was going to do me no good. He was a decent man once, but now... now he was nothing. Just a pile of shit that thought too much of himself.

Kristin stood up from the chair she was sitting on and padded to me.

She peered outside, but also couldn't see if someone was keeping a close eye on her place - on us.

"I don't care what your decision regarding him is, but whatever happens, I want you to know that I've got your back."

She turned her head to me and I couldn't help but hug her. Her pulsing warmth to me was all I needed to reaffirm the fact I could trust her, no matter what happened.

And David... I didn't even know if he was going to come back to Le Kissr or not. I just hoped he wasn't going to.

I didn't want to see his face, even if part of me was fighting against me - trying to convince me that, maybe, he'd been keeping those things hidden from me because he needed to keep me safe.

That was bullshit. It had to be.

* * *

His eyes looked at me like he couldn't believe this was happening. Oisin had always thought I would end up working for him for the rest of my life. He'd never thought I would become his number one hostess. I brought more money into his business than all the other hostesses combined, and that was saying something, considering how experienced so many of them were.

But there was something they could never compete against me – looks. I had the looks, and clients of all backgrounds and ages showed up here just for the chance of meeting me for the first time.

He sighed and said, "You really don't think you can work here a little more? We could pay you all you need, and some more too. We are more than willing to keep you here for as long as possible."

I smiled. I knew that his proposal was a good one, but I couldn't accept it. I didn't need his club anymore. How things changed all of sudden for him, right? He'd once thought he had me wrapped around his finger.

Oisin had thought I was really going to end up being forced to work for him for the rest of my life.

"No, I just really need to begin a new life and forget this whole thing ever happened. Maybe you thought I was going to have a different opinion of your club, but I'm also not one to lie. I didn't like working here – at all."

"Fair enough," he said, standing up. When he offered me his hand, he continued, "Thanks for working with us for as long as you could, though. You taught so many of my hostesses valuable lessons they are going to keep with them for the rest of their lives."

I smiled.

"I don't think they care much anyway. They are just happy I'm finally leaving."

He chuckled. There was no denying Le Kissr was never going to be the same again without me. I changed a lot of things here, even if not many of the hostesses liked how I worked. Most of them were jubilant I was never going to show up here again.

Oisin took me to the door. Opening it, his eyes held me for a moment. I could tell he was thinking he was wishing he could tell me something – anything – to make me change my mind. but there was nothing that could be said.

"I just want to say it was an honor having you working here, Renae."

I couldn't say the same, but I was still going to be polite to him. No point in being an ass all of sudden. He was the only person that thought I deserved another loan, after all.

"It's okay. You are going to find someone else that wants to work for you and replace me."

He chuckled one more time. "I don't think it will be that easy."

"Maybe not, but you are the kind of person that doesn't give up easily. It's all going to sort itself out for you."

"You are right, I don't give up easily. Still wish I could make you change your mind," he said before chatting with me some more and then closing the door.

When I walked out of there, I remembered I didn't make any friends in the building. The club was still never going to forget me, though.

* * *

I shouldn't be doing this. I should be stronger than this, but I just... couldn't stop my mind. it couldn't stop thinking about him. it thought of him all the time, and that was maddening. It made me feel like hating myself – and it managed to do just so.

I hated myself right now, going to his profile on Instagram to figure out if our break up was affecting his wellbeing or not. It sure as hell seemed it wasn't, though, considering he hadn't... posted anything since I found out what he'd been hiding from me this whole time.

I still didn't know what happened to Troy, and the fact I ended up not calling the police... made me hate myself even more. Now that I was thinking about it, I should have done it. I should have called the police on his ass.

That would have taught him I wasn't someone to be messed around with.

I could hear the sound of the cars driving on the road, making me remember I was still at Kristin's. I was so thankful she allowed me to live here for the time being. Such a considerate friend she was.

She was the only friend I had. Other people I knew didn't care about me enough.

She liked David when she met him for the first time, but now she knew what he was really like. Behind the mask he put on to make other people think he was a good man.

What a lie.

What a fucking lie.

He didn't post any new photo of his online, though I couldn't help but notice that more people followed him now. Women of all ages drooled over him, commenting on his older photos regarding his sudden disappearance.

Damn. Those women were obsessed with David, and their obsession made me feel more obsessed too. I was holding my phone in my hands and thinking about shooting a message to him.

Now that I left the hostess club, he was never going to see me again. Or maybe that was reason enough for him to attend the club more often now. I asked some people around there, and they told me he'd been going to Le Kissr still. He'd just been... seeing some other girls. Seeing some other women that sucked up to him and didn't have the baggage of feelings I now had.

His face still looked so kissable, and I couldn't help but remember all the good times we shared. I scrolled down, checking more of his photos out, and finding out yet again I loved the guy too much and just couldn't stop thinking about him.

I'd almost hoped Kristin would just open the door of the room and step in, get the phone from me and give me a sermon while saying that, "I shouldn't be allowed to have a phone anymore because it's making me feel miserable."

And if she were to do that, she would be right. Having easy access to the internet was making me feel depressed, though one of the things I'd told myself I would never feel was depression. That was the kind of thing that killed my uncle, and I still... remembered him like he was right here with me.

He was one of the family members I most loved.

The warm blanket was the only impeding me from feeling like killing myself right now. It was getting cold outside, and inside here, too. Winter was coming. Christmas was coming and it was going to be the worst ever in my life.

Going through such a period about remembrance, friendship, love, and the like without my boyfriend and parents wasn't how I thought things were going to turn out to be like this year. I'd thought I would have someone else other than Kristin with me.

She was such a nice friend. She'd promised I could continue living here for the foreseeable future. Kristin had mentioned – and she was right – that it would be terrible for my mental health if I lived alone, in my house, while thinking all the time – and growing paranoid about it – that there was someone outside tailing me.

Keeping tabs on me.

But some weeks had passed since the last time I met David, and nothing happened. Nothing at all. Could it be that David had lied when he said he was going to have someone keeping tabs on me? I didn't know if he lied, but now that I was thinking about the possibility...

Perhaps he did, but that didn't matter. What mattered was that he'd threatened me and just... gave up on the beautiful relationship we'd cultivated for months.

I sighed and checked out some more of his photos online. They showed him holding meetings, talking to important-looking people, smiling, laughing, and the like. He was the perfect specimen for LinkedIn's fakeness.

And he had a profile there too, now that I was thinking about it. But over there he didn't have many of his photos of him. Over there, I couldn't satiate my need to see him in person. Checking his photos on Instagram was still not the best way to do that – the only way to do so was by meeting the man in person – but it was still... something.

It was still something I needed to do.

I killed the screen of my phone. I was going to have a full day tomorrow, or today. It didn't matter. Going to college, doing the finals, and that sort of thing. And if it happened again, if I met him one more time, then I would prove him he was wrong.

I wasn't someone he could play around with.

* * *

The place looked especially beautiful this morning. People of all backgrounds and ages sat on the chairs placed on the grass. The architecture of the college still looked pleasantly old – old, but it was still clear that people took care of it. It was mostly gray and it gave off the vibe that, on the inside, it looked more like a castle.

And it sure as hell did.

I was with all the other girls that were going to get their certificates at the end of the ceremony. Professors and students chatted, and were having fun, laughing, and so on and so forth. The atmosphere was like an intense buzz that could be a little overwhelming for people that don't like loud noises, but it wasn't the case with me. I reveled in it.

I took a look to the side and thought how beautiful the trees looked. These maple trees gave the college a different charm. I wished my neighborhood had more of them.

Kristin stood on the other side of where the ceremony was being held, looking as beautiful as ever. We talked a lot before coming here, and I couldn't help but feel like going to her right now.

But I knew that would be wrong.

The ceremony was going to start soon and she wouldn't like it if I brought unnecessary attention unto myself.

She had an updo hair that really highlighted the best qualities of her face. She was short and a little on the chubby side, but still knew how to look her best for occasions like this one. It turned out, though, that she couldn't do the same when she was in her apartment. Couldn't care less about what she looked like when strangers weren't seeing her.

I sighed.

My thoughts went straight back to David. I had no idea what he was doing with his life now, though If I were to guess, I'd say he was probably having the time of his life. The time of his life without me, without a woman he couldn't care less about. It used to be different, but since I got too curious-

And I wasn't going to change my mind about that. I did the right thing. I knew I did.

"It's time for the start of the ceremony, so now, if you'll all excuse me."

An old man was standing on the wooden platform now, a microphone in front of his face. He cleared his throat and began to recite the words that described our college. They were supposed to be about friendship, hardship, facing own's fears, and that sort of thing, but to be honest, I couldn't care less about those things right now.

They didn't mean much to me, and it wasn't like this college's administration did good on those words anyway. They didn't follow it.

Kristin looked jubilant when I was called to stand on the platform, where I was going to grab my certificate and then walk out of here with my head held high – as if while studying here, I didn't end up working as a hostess and met the only guy that truly made me feel like a woman. Not even Troy had managed to make me feel like that.

Though I didn't want to admit it, I could still feel as if his arms were wrapped around me, pulling me to him and grinding his groin against my butt. I shook my head. No point in thinking about those things at this moment.

I grabbed the certificate and read out loud the words on the letter. I'd written just for this occasion, though I didn't put much thought into it. I just wrote sentences I thought these people were going to like to listen to during this fine, sunny morning.

I lifted my head and that was when my eyes landed on *him*. They landed on David, who was standing behind the crowd. He had his hands in his pockets and a look on his face that told me a lot of things, and not all of them were positive.

I froze there and then, someone patting me on the shoulder to tell me I needed to get off the platform and head to where all the other former students were going to – where they were taking photos of themselves holding their certificates and that sort of thing.

And I did that, though not without looking at him all the time, staring at him. When I was stepping on the grass again, I rushed ahead, pushing my weight through some people that grunted and complained, but when I got to where he was, he was nowhere to be seen.

I looked from side to side, but couldn't even see his car, and that was one of the many things about him I was never going to forget.

Kristin stood behind me, patting me on the shoulder as well. "Did something happen? You look like you just saw a ghost."

"It's David. I think he was here."

Her eyes widened.

"David? What? Are you sure about that? You didn't just see a man that looks like him, but isn't him, right?"

I shook my head.

"No. That was not it. I'm pretty sure it was him."

Her lips trembled.

"He couldn't have come here. This ceremony is for family and friends only."

She was right, but I knew what I'd seen. I wasn't going to pretend otherwise. David was here, and he was watching my ceremony. But why did he do that? For what purpose? It didn't make any sense to me.

Kristin grabbed my hand and said, "C'mon. We need to take some pictures of you holding the certificate and show all those assholes you don't like that you managed to do it, that you graduated."

I smiled. At least there was something good to take away from all this, but still... David's sudden apparition was something I was going to think about all the time from now on.

Chapter 10

I turned and tossed in the bed, hating myself for the fact I was thinking about him. Thinking about David. I'd thought that his apparition had been nothing more than a joke from my imagination – I'd eventually learned to think that. But now... now I couldn't stop thinking about it. Thinking about him. His eyes meeting mine, his hands looking for mine, the heat of his body, and the comfort it brought to me.

I needed those things, now more than ever.

And still, I wasn't about to go grabbing my phone and dialing his number. I knew that would be the wrong thing to do, and I didn't want him thinking he'd won - that he made me so desperate for his love I was willing to forget what he did.

He killed Troy.

That's what I heard. I heard about it not too long ago. Of course, news outlets didn't report the death of a young man they didn't care about.

But I still head about it, through his parents. The thought that they called me just to tell me that sickened me a little. We didn't even talk about it properly. They just rang my number and then ended the call like it had been nothing more than an obligation for them.

David had so much to explain to me now, and I really wished to find out what it was that was happening in his life.

Why he'd been acting like that the whole time we'd been together.

I grabbed my phone and turned on the screen one more time. I didn't go to his profile on Instagram. No way I was going to do that. What I did was to delete my profile so that it would stop bothering me.

Keeping it would mean thinking about him all the time and remembering that I could always just go to his profile to check out some of his photos. I didn't want to do that. I was tired of that, and it didn't add anything to my life anyway, other than making me feel more miserable.

I didn't want to admit it, but I was thinking that maybe I might have to go to a therapist. It could be the only way to properly forget the guy once and for all.

I finished deleting my account and felt relief washing over my heart. That was pretty much the only thing about him I still had. Nothing else on the phone. No pictures, nothing of the sort. David was like a dead man to me now.

I wished he was dead or living on the other side of the planet so that I could stop thinking that we were going to meet up one day, somewhere.

I guessed it just wasn't meant to be.

* * *

I sat on a chair in front of the office, wondering what the interview was going to be like. I graduated in administration, so I was hoping I was going to land this opportunity. The chance to help run one of the most important companies in the country wasn't something many people out there could ever have.

Through some connections, luck, and my resume, I managed to get selected for an interview here. An interview I had no idea how it was going to be like. I just hoped I wasn't about to make a fool of myself.

The corridor that was the waiting room was rather cold, and I didn't know if that was something I was just feeling or if it truly was colder than normal. The heater was turned on, of course, and the wind was howling on the outside of the building. It felt rather chilly too, especially with the snowflakes that began to fall.

It wouldn't be long now until the end of the year. I had Christmas without my parents, inside Kristin's apartment. It was sad and it made me feel happy at the same time. Hopeful too, I guess. Kristin always managed to make me laugh, even when her jokes were pretty out-of-touch.

The door that led to the interview room opened and out of it stepped a man. Just a guy about my age that had come here seeking to claim that opportunity too. Though I didn't know him, I was already feeling I'd lost to him already. He looked so confident, especially with how he strode forward.

I took a deep breath and stood up. No point in thinking that sort of thing when my interview was going to start soon. Walking to the room, I stopped when I stood right at the doorway. What I was seeing... It couldn't be true. I had to be seeing things again.

It was David, sitting on the other side of his desk as he looked at me while supporting his head on his hands. His eyes looked at me with a curious intent, and I couldn't tell what it was he was thinking about right now.

I cleared my throat and walked into the room, my hand closing the door behind me. I had no idea what was going on here, but I was more than willing to find out. His presence, his eyes, everything else about him made me feel uncomfortable, but if he was here – and he was – then that meant he knew I was coming.

And considering that, then it wouldn't be too far-fetched to think that he needed to talk to me.

For what reason, what he was thinking we needed to talk about, I didn't know, but again, I was going to find out.

I'd spent this whole time – months – without talking to him. Without thinking about him, and now there he stood, sitting behind his desk like he was the most important businessman in the whole country.

He lifted his head from his hands, putting them on the table, and said, "Renae. I know this might look odd and curious, but believe me when I tell you I meant for this meeting to happen."

"What?"

My voice betrayed my anger and how incredulous about this whole thing I felt. I felt betrayed. Betrayed by the people that selected me for this job opportunity, that didn't tell me he was going to be the interviewer, that-

Stop, Renae. They didn't know you once had a relationship with that asshole that was reclining on his chair now.

He stood up from his chair and padded to me. "I don't know how to go about this. You know I am not very good with words."

"That is putting it mildly," I said, crossing my arms over my chest.

Was I really okay going on with this? Shouldn't I just march out of the room and pretend that nothing of this ever happened? Shouldn't I just imagine he didn't even exist?

The thought of doing those things tempted me, but something inside me was telling me to continue listening to him. I needed to find out why he pulled this off, why he fooled me into thinking this was going to be nothing more than an interview.

"I know this is all sorts of wrong, but I needed to see you one more time, and to tell you that I am... sorry about the way I treated you."

I took a step back, putting more distance between him and me.

"Sorry? You are sorry you had one of your goons tailing me all the time? Keeping tabs on me like I was some kind of criminal?"

He shook his head.

"I didn't do that. I changed my mind as soon as you walked out on me."

My heart skipped a beat. I wasn't going to let this asshole change my mind about him. He was still that – nothing more than a jerk. My opinion of him wasn't going to change.

And he couldn't have lied about it. He wouldn't pull something as stupid as that. I was sure of it. David was many things, but he wasn't stupid. And most of all, he isn't going to begin thinking I am some kind of idiot that can be fooled. I am not going to accept his apology.

"I don't believe that. I saw someone following me."

"You were seeing things. I didn't have anyone following you. I trusted you."

I widened my eyes, shock coursing through my heart. "You what? You 'trusted' me? You think I'm going to believe something like that?"

"At least I didn't do it like you. You didn't trust me when I walked out of our home that night."

He was right. I could have trusted him then and everything would be alright now. Everything would be fine and he and I would be living a life like no other. But the man that warned me about David did so looking pretty serious about it, and I couldn't ignore it.

His eyes still looked at me with a sense of longing, love, and curiosity I couldn't ignore. David wasn't on the right here, but he was making me think that, maybe, our relationship could get another chance.

I just wasn't sure if I wanted that or not.

"That doesn't excuse anything. You were pretty rude when you found out I was in that building."

"You were spying on me. How would you have felt if the roles had been reserved?"

I opened my mouth, but shut it a moment later. He was right. I would have felt pretty pissed off, too. Not as pissed as he did, though. Probably more. A lot more. I wouldn't have used words as kind as he did if that had occurred. If he'd been the one spying on me.

I turned my head to the side a little, refusing to look into his eyes. With my arms crossed over my chest, I was telling him I wasn't going to budge. I'm not going to admit he is right about anything. That would be all he needed to make it so I would never be able to forget him.

And I didn't want to have to go through another sleepless night because of him. I was tired of that sort of thing, and I didn't need it in my life again.

"That still doesn't excuse the fact you've been lying about your business to me this whole time. You should have just told me about it."

"And why would I have done that when it would have meant you walking out on me?"

"I should have done that a long time ago," I said, breathing out. "Actually, I shouldn't have let you into my life – ever. That was the worst mistake I made."

"It was no mistake."

"It was."

He exhaled, still keeping his distance from me. good. I didn't want to have to run away from him screaming. I didn't want to bring more attention to myself.

"You killed Troy," I accused.

His eyes shot wide.

"What?"

"You killed him, and don't try to lie about it. I know you did. His parents told me he died."

"I didn't kill him. He was fine when I let him out. As fine as he could be, that is."

I turned my head to him, studying his expression. He looked genuinely surprised by my accusation, like he couldn't believe I was telling him something like that. Troy's parents couldn't have lied to me when they told me about it. Something was off here, and I didn't like it one bit.

"You are lying to me, again."

"I'm not lying. But... there's no way I can prove it to you, other than the look of shock on my face."

He was right about that last thing. He did look shocked, though I knew better than to use that kind of conclusion to begin thinking he was being genuine for once. This whole time he'd been keeping the truth about him – his other income source – hidden behind many locked doors, after all.

And it did tell me I needed to be careful around him.

And I didn't know why I cared that much about it, considering how much of an asshole Troy turned out to be. Kidnapping me and then trying to use me as bait? But that was me looking at it through just one angle.

Looking at the issue from another angle, this wasn't just about Troy. But about David as well. I'd always thought David was a good man – deep down there. If he killed someone... I wouldn't know what to think of it.

Most of all, I wouldn't continue standing here, pretending we were having a normal conversation.

He approached me some more, and I didn't step away from him. I wasn't going to show him he struck fear in my heart. No way I was going to allow that to happen.

"Renae, you need to trust me on this."

Maybe I should trust him, considering Troy's parents didn't tell me how he died. They were pretty brief about it. All they did was to tell me he'd passed away and that that was that. They didn't tell me if it had been from wounds, bullets, or something like that. I should have probed the issue further, explored it with them when they were on the phone with me.

But now... now was a bit too late for that.

I shook my head. "I don't think it matters anyway, David. You shouldn't have faked this whole interview thing. I'd thought I was actually going to have a chance to work here and make it in life."

"But I can do that, for you. I can hire you and allow you to work here, for me."

"I should have called the police on you. That would have ended this whole thing."

This was all wringing my heart, and I couldn't help but feel like kissing him. I knew that would be the wrong thing to do. It would send the wrong message, but I still couldn't help but feel like doing that.

I knew he was willing – willing to do that. But still... it would ruin this whole thing, and I was feeling we were progressing toward something here. What that something was, I didn't know, but I was soon going to find out.

"You know that would have solved nothing," he told me.

"Maybe not, but it would still have made me feel better about it."

He took a deep breath, his hand looking for mine. "Renae... all I need is another chance. Nothing more than that. You don't need to work here. You don't need to ever work in your life again, though you do make a pretty beautiful hostess."

I let a smile flash on my face. Dammit! This wasn't how this was supposed to go down. I wasn't supposed to be letting him hold my hand like this, almost making me feel like I was in the wrong here.

I wasn't. I was making the right choice and doing the right thing. David had already proven he didn't deserve my love. And giving him another chance? Did he think I was stupid or something like that?"

I took a deep breath. I knew he didn't deserve my love. I knew it like I knew the back of my hand, but the truth was... that love is blind and that I just couldn't stop thinking about him. All those sleepless nights thinking about him all the time, remembering the moments we shared... Those things were deeply ingrained in my mind.

And his lips, his hand, his whole body kept melting me more and more for him. I couldn't resist it, so I ended up pulling him to me and kissing him. I wasn't going to mention anything about working here, though. It would be too awkward.

I was going to find another place, another company. Anything would be better than working under the man that'd said he loved me but had done so many things to prove me otherwise.

When I pulled away, he had a big smile on his face.

"I knew you were going to change your mind," he said, looking as cocky as ever.

I wasn't going to deny it. One of the things I most loved about him was his bad-boy attitude. That was something most men out there didn't have, and he seemed to sport that to perfection.

His other hand grabbed mine, the comfort he was making me feel more than enough to make it seem he could keep me safe from everything and anything in the world.

"I didn't change my mind. I'm only... I guess maybe giving you the second-chance you are looking for."

He took me to the balcony of the apartment building we were in, and we looked out on the city. The buzz of the city reminded me of Le Kissr, where I'd met David. Enough time passed since our incident to haze the memories I had of how he treated me.

And love is a funny thing, right? Sometimes, it doesn't matter how the other soul mistreated you. All that matters is knowing they're the person you've been looking for this whole time.

The only one that can make you feel complete.

His hand squeezed mine, and without thinking about it too hard, he pulled me to him. We shared another kiss, and it was one of the many I was never going to forget. A kiss from David... the only man I truly cared about.

There were still many things with him to be resolved but I was sure that, in time, they were going to be.

Epilogue

He stood tall in front of me. One of the tallest men I'd seen my whole life. He was probably around 6 foot 3 or something like that – a head taller than me, in other terms. With his hands holding me, he made me feel so safe it was almost impossible to describe it. The heat of his body was enough to make it seem there wasn't even a world around me.

No surroundings. Just the man I needed to make my life complete.

And here I'd thought that giving him another chance was going to be a mistake. How wrong I'd been about that. It turned out to be the best thing I could have chosen for my life.

Did he prove the things I thought he did he didn't do? No, he didn't, but I just ended up dropping the issue altogether anyway and focused on how he was making me feel. And he did good on his word when he told me he was going to make me feel loved again.

Or maybe I should say I never stopped loving the man. I'd never stopped checking out his profile on Instagram, after all.

We were lounging on the beach, the sound of the crashing waves tickling my ears. His hand looked for mine. He gave it a squeeze when my eyes settled on his big, growing bulge. I'd thought what it would be like to have sex with him on the beach. Would that be something he would be okay with?

And what sort of question was even that. Of course he would be okay with it.

I knew he would.

His lips approached mine again, and we kissed. The heat of his body traveled to mine, hardening my nipples. I wore nothing more than a swimsuit that kept my belly exposed. His hand played with my breasts, and I could tell he was thinking about it.

Thinking what it would be like if we fucked here.

And I couldn't help but think about his cock. It was big, hard, and so veiny. Hmmmm. Just the thought of putting that thing in my mouth again was enough to make me drool. While we kissed, I drooled and drooled some more.

I couldn't stop thinking about his white seeds filling me to the brim. More than anything, that's what I needed right now.

He ended the kiss, his eyes looking at me through his sunglasses. I couldn't see his eyes per se, but I still knew they were looking at me. Looking at me and wondering what I was feeling at the moment.

And now, more than ever before, I needed to confirm his suspicions about me.

"You are looking so hot right now," I told him.

"And you as well, my princess."

"My princess? What is this now? Some kind of age-play kinky stuff?"

He smiled. "Something like that."

I couldn't help but get off the lounge chair and sit right on top of his groin region, feeling his big, hard cock pressing against my pussy. He didn't get me pregnant that night we had sex for the first time, and now that I was thinking about it... I wished he'd done it.

This vacation on the beach would be so much better if I were holding his baby in my arms.

"You are going to make me regret bringing you here," he said.

"For what reason?"

"Getting you pregnant without your permission."

"But you do have my permission. You don't think that is enough?"

"So, I have your permission and everything?" he questioned before pushing me off him and forcing me to lie down on the sand. It was hot and it stuck to my skin, but I didn't mind it much.

I was having the moment of my life with him and, for me, that was all that mattered right now.

His hand grabbed my neck, squeezing the skin. "I could kill you right now, and it would all be fine. I could dump your body in the ocean, and nobody would ever find out about it. What do you have to say in your defense?"

"That I'm not afraid of you."

"Really? Not afraid of me? That is not something I can let slide," he said before ripping off my swimsuit – he was just that strong – and then taking off his clothes.

We were on the beach, but this island was a private one. Nobody lived here, other than us. We could do everything and anything here, and no one would find out about it. This place was just so serene, especially with the waves crashing against the shore, the squawking of the seagulls, and the heat of the sun kissing my chocolate-skin.

"Fuck me right now, and don't hold anything back," I begged him, getting a smile from his stubbly face.

"That I can do, my princess," he said before easing himself right in, his cock stretching my tunnel to its limits, his gland going all the way and reaching my g-spot. I moaned then and there, feeling him inside me, his balls touching my skin.

"Please..." I begged him.

"Please... what?" He asked, kissing my neck, nibbing it, and making it seem like this thing was going to take much more time than I'd thought it was going to.

He pounded in and out of me. Sweat broke out on his forehead as the rest of his body shone under the light of the sun. His balls slapped against my butt, and I could feel as if this was going to cross a line I'd never thought possible before.

But that.. was nothing more than me having a vivid imagination. This was taking the right path.

It didn't take him long to finish creaming inside me, his cum hot and very sticky. He pulled out and then lounged back on his beach chair that looked more like a single bed.

For a moment, I wished that chair of his was big and good enough for both of us to lie on it. When we got here, that hadn't been something we thought about.

The sun began to set. I turned my head to him and asked, "I need your babies inside my belly. That would make my life feel so complete."

"Renae, you are going to have them and so many more too. In fact, you are going to have so many babies inside that belly of yours it will feel weird when you don't have them in you anymore."

I smiled. We finished sipping our coconut water and then headed back to the medium-sized house that was not too far from the beach.

After getting inside it, he made me my favorite food. Lasagna. The smell wafted in the air, making me sniff to appreciate it that much more.

He must have cooked one of the best lasagnas in the whole world.

When I headed to the kitchen, I devoured so many slices my belly was full. We then went to the couch and I slept on his lap.

His hand caressed my head while I closed my eyes and fell asleep. All I could feel was the heat of his body and how soft it was.

He wore nothing, as usual. The turned-on TV made it pretty easy for me not to think about anything when falling asleep – and that was the best way of going about it.

Even though I couldn't be sure about it, I knew the months and days ahead held a lot in store for us. And for the most part, they were going to be good.

The things we were going to do together. I couldn't stop thinking about them.

There were so many plans to fulfill and places to visit...

The End

But before you go, I want to thank you for having read the whole book. Your support means a lot to me. Each book reveals something different about myself, and I hope you enjoyed reading it as much as I enjoyed writing it.

As one last little thing, I'd like to request you to leave a review for this book on the Amazon store page (or just how many stars you think it deserves). It doesn't take long, and your opinion is very valuable to me. I know some of you leave your reviews on Goodreads, but on Amazon is where they have more visibility, and you'd be helping me a lot too.

More from Me

Mafia Vassal: A Dark Italian Mafia Romance Bundle
Beg Me: An Arranged Marriage Dark Mafia Romance
Don't Cry: A Secret Baby Dark Mafia Romance
Seizing her Heart: A Bratva Mafia Romance Collection
Conquering my Queen: A Dark Mafia Romance Bundle
Challenging Destiny: An Arranged Marriage Dark Mafia Romance
Chaining my Queen: A Secret Baby Dark Mafia Romance
Hell is Crying: A Secret Baby Mafia Romance
Beyond Forgiving: A Dark Mafia Captive Romance
Chosen to be Mine: A Dark Arranged Marriage Mafia Romance
Have no Fear: An Enemies to Lovers Academy Romance
Under his Mercy: A Dark High School Bully Romance
Lure Me: A Dark High School Bully Romance
Fallen Angel: A Dark High School Bully Romance
Stop Lying: A Dark High School and College Bundle
Stop Running: A Dark High School Bully Romance
Take Control: A Dark High School Bully Romance
Wounded Soldier: A BBW Romance
Venom Curves: A BBW Alpha Male Romance
Impossibly Curvy: A BBW Alpha Male
Wild Curves: A Western BBW Alpha Male Instalove Romance
Unfair Curves: A BBW Alpha Male Romance
Sempre Minha: Um Romance Macho Alfa

About the Author

Jolie Damman lives with her puppies and many cats on her farmland. She enjoys spending time with nature and tending to her property. When she has some free time, which doesn't happen as often as she would like, she writes her books.

As a writer, she hopes to touch and change the heart of her readers. Her books are not for those weak of the heart, and they tend to be spicier than most. One word after the other, she doesn't stop typing until she has written her idea, and she is very desire-driven when it comes to establishing the connections of her characters.